"I require your services for longer."

Maddie's eyes narrowed. "How much longer?"

Remi hesitated, simply because he hadn't considered this. How long? Long enough to appease his people? His own desire for her?

The latter would scorch itself out sooner rather than later. The hotter the passion, the quicker it burned out, right?

Which left only the well-being of his people. They'd been through one scandal in the recent past. Montegova required stability. Not one that would cost him a lifetime but for the foreseeable future nevertheless.

"Remi? What sort of solution?" There was apprehension in her voice but also hope.

Those same emotions he'd felt when confronted with Celeste's diagnosis. The outcome would be different this time, both for her father and for his own expectations as the ruler of Montegova.

The twinge dissipated, and he breathed easier. "I'll ensure your father receives the treatment he needs to get him back onto his feet. You'd need never worry about him again."

She took an unsteady breath. "And in return?" she pressed again.

"In return, I want you to marry me."

Conveniently Wed!

Conveniently wedded, passionately bedded!

Whether there's a debt to be paid, a will to be obeyed or a business to be saved...she's got no choice but to say, "I do!"

But these billionaire bridegrooms have got another think coming if they imagine marriage will be that easy...

Soon their convenient brides become the objects of inconvenient desire!

Find out what happens after the vows in:

The Greek's Bought Bride by Sharon Kendrick

Claiming His Wedding Night Consequence by Abby Green

Bound by a One-Night Vow by Melanie Milburne

Sicilian's Bride for a Price by Tara Pammi

Claiming His Christmas Wife by Dani Collins

My Bought Virgin Wife by Caitlin Crews

The Sicilian's Bought Cinderella by Michelle Smart

Look for more Conveniently Wed! titles coming soon!

Maya Blake

CROWN PRINCE'S BOUGHT BRIDE

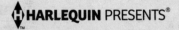 HARLEQUIN PRESENTS®

Recycling programs
for this product may
not exist in your area.

ISBN-13: 978-1-335-47811-5

Crown Prince's Bought Bride

First North American publication 2019

Copyright © 2019 by Maya Blake

This edition published by arrangement with Harlequin Books S.A.

For questions and comments about the quality of this book, please contact us at CustomerService@Harlequin.com.

Printed in U.S.A.

www.Harlequin.com

Maya Blake's hopes of becoming a writer were born when she picked up her first romance at thirteen. Little did she know her dream would come true! Does she still pinch herself every now and then to make sure it's not a dream? Yes, she does! Feel free to pinch her, too, via Twitter, Facebook or Goodreads! Happy reading!

Books by Maya Blake

Harlequin Presents

A Diamond Deal with the Greek
Signed Over to Santino
Pregnant at Acosta's Demand
The Sultan Demands His Heir
His Mistress by Blackmail

One Night With Consequences

The Boss's Nine-Month Negotiation

Secret Heirs of Billionaires

Brunetti's Secret Son

Rival Brothers

A Deal with Alejandro
One Night with Gael

Bound to the Desert King

Sheikh's Pregnant Cinderella

Visit the Author Profile page
at Harlequin.com for more titles.

CHAPTER ONE

REMIREZ ALEXANDER MONTEGOVA, Crown Prince of the Kingdom of Montegova, paused before the imposing double doors, his raised fist as frozen as the rest of his body.

It didn't escape him that anyone who knew him would be shocked by this uncharacteristic display of hesitancy. Since infancy he'd been lauded as a fearless, valiant visionary who would one day steer his people to greater heights than any of his forebears had imagined.

But here he was, cowed by a set of doors.

Granted, they weren't just any doors. They were the portals to his final destiny. As pretentious as the words sounded, that didn't make them any less true.

He'd been dreading this day.

The simple truth was he didn't want to go inside. Didn't want to face his mother the Queen. Every instinct warned him that he wouldn't emerge the same person.

When had that ever mattered? He'd never belonged to himself. He belonged to history. To the destiny forged by countless Mongetovan warriors who'd fought bloody battles to carve out this Western Mediterranean kingdom with their bare hands.

For as long as he drew breath he would belong to

the people of Montegova. Duty and destiny. Two words branded with indelible ink into his skin.

Like twin weights they settled like a heavy cloak over his shoulders, making his next breath a torturous chore.

'Your Highness?' his senior aide prompted nervously but firmly from behind him. 'Her Majesty is waiting.'

One voice in many that peppered his daily life. One that cajoled and coaxed and, when he closed himself off to that, as he'd mastered doing, prodded and pushed.

The morning's summons, however, had been absolute.

His mother requested his presence at nine o'clock sharp. The solid gold antique clock standing proudly in one of the many marbled and hallowed hallways of the Grand Palace of Montegova solemnly announced that he was five seconds from being late.

With a resigned breath, he unfroze his fist, rapped sharply on the gold-leaf-framed doors and awaited the command to enter.

It arrived, brisk and firm, yet wrapped in a layer of unmistakable warmth.

The voice accurately reflected the woman seated in the throne-like chair beneath the grand coat of arms that spelled out her royal status in Latin, her flint-grey gaze tracking him across the vast office.

She nodded approvingly when he executed a respectful bow before taking his seat before her.

'I was wondering how long you'd remain behind the door. Am I really so frightful?' she mused with a trace of sadness in her eyes.

That sadness grated, but Remi refused to let it show.

He was used to people wearing that expression in his presence. He was used to several more expressions, yet sorrow and pity chafed the worst. But he supposed it was better than being treated as if he were made of fragile glass.

He ignored the emotion and searched her face for signs that, just this once, his instincts were wrong. But from her perfectly coiffed hair and flawless make-up, to the classic Chanel suit she favoured for official duties, and the diamond and emerald brooch made in the image of the Montegovan flag, Remi was left in no doubt that this meeting was exactly what he'd suspected it to be.

The axe was truly about to fall.

'Not frightful, no. But I suspect the reason for this summoning will leave one of us less than thrilled.'

His mother's lips pursed momentarily before she rose. A tall, striking woman, she would have commanded attention with effortless ease even if she hadn't been the reigning Montegovan monarch. Long before she'd become Queen she'd won three beauty pageants across the world. When she deigned to bestow it on the deserving her smile could stop a grown man in his tracks—Remi had seen it first-hand. The hair that had turned silver almost overnight ten years ago, after his father's death, had once been as dark as his own, but she'd owned that very visible sign of pain and grief with the same stalwart strength that had stopped her kingdom from descending into chaos at the sudden death of its King and the scandal that had followed. At twenty-three, Remi had been deemed too young to take the throne so his mother had taken his place as interim ruler. He was supposed to take the throne on his thirtieth birthday. But then further tragedy had struck.

His mother was the strongest woman he knew. Which was why everything inside him tightened when, after several minutes examining the spectacular view from her office window, she returned to her desk, planted her palms on the polished antique cherry wood and locked eyes with him.

'It's time, Remirez.'

His gut clenched tighter. She very rarely used his full first name. As a child that had never boded well for him or his hide. As a grown man of thirty-two it still commanded his attention.

Unable to remain seated in the foreboding of impending fate, he stood and paced in front of her desk. 'How much time are we talking, here? Weeks? Months?'

It wouldn't be years. She'd already given him two years. And lately she'd indicated, without cruelty, that it was time to set his own grief aside.

'I would like to make the announcement that I'm stepping down at the next Solstice Festival.'

The third week in June.

'That's…three months away.' The reality of it hit him like a cold wave in the face.

'Yes,' she replied firmly. 'Which means time is of the essence. We must put our house in order before we begin to make the announcements.'

'Announcements?' he echoed. 'Plural?'

His mother's gaze dropped momentarily to her desk. 'I'm not just stepping down, Remi. I'm also taking extended leave from all official duties.'

Isadora Montegova wasn't just the ruling monarch, she was also an active member of parliament.

'You're resigning? Why?'

Her lips compressed—a sign that she didn't like to admit whatever it was she was about to say. 'The past few years have been difficult for both of us. I need a little…time away from everything.'

She wouldn't stoop so low as to call it *me time*, the way others might, but if anyone had earned the right to retreat and regroup it was his mother.

Not only had she borne the unexpected death of her husband with unwavering strength, she'd weathered the subsequent scandal unleashed by the discovery of her husband's decades-long secret with remarkable dignity and poise.

Behind closed doors, though, Remi had caught glimpses of the true toll it had taken on her. He himself had barely been able to hold back his fury at discovering that the father he'd held in such high esteem had proved to be faithless. Over the years his rage had boiled down to a simmering resentment, but it had never dissipated. Because not only had his father caused his mother untold hardship by his actions, he'd also thrown the kingdom into turmoil for years. Years which had taken a brutal toll on his mother. On him and on Zak, his younger brother.

Secrets and lies. It was a cliché until it happened on your doorstep and was played out for the world to see.

He tamped down on his fury as his mother reached out.

'Which brings me to the next housekeeping problem.' She opened a slim folder and slid it across the desk.

And there, displayed in full Technicolor, was the latest source of his mother's angst.

Jules Montegova.

The surly half-brother who'd been presented to them moments after his father's burial. The twenty-eight-year-old whose paternity had been proven via a discreet

DNA test, to be royal, courtesy of an illicit affair his father had indulged in when he had briefly been stationed in Paris on diplomatic duty.

Jules was the scandal that had nearly unsettled the kingdom. The paparazzi had gone on a feeding frenzy for months, prising open every closet they could find in the hope of unearthing more skeletons.

It would have been easier to stomach had Jules not proved to be nothing but a thorn in their sides from the moment he'd arrived in Montegova ten years ago.

Remi scanned the picture, his jaw clenching as he noted the glassy eyes, the dishevelment, the slurred expression of drunkenness. 'What has he done now?' he bit out.

Queen Isadora's mouth twisted. 'A less aggravating question would be what *hasn't* he done? Three weeks ago it was reckless gambling in Monte Carlo, then he flew to Paris and carried on gambling for another four days. The royal bursar was apoplectic when he received the bill. Ten days ago he turned up in Barcelona and gatecrashed a private party Duke Armando was throwing for his niece. Since then he's been in London, and in the past few days in *this* woman's company,' she said, sliding aside the first picture to reveal several more.

They all showed variations of the same woman. Dark blonde. Leggy. Bright green eyes and a figure designed to stop traffic. She was striking. And her smile would win a contest against a thousand-watt bulb.

But she was a dime a dozen in Remi's world. All flash and no substance.

Hell, in one picture she was literally flashing her underwear, uncaring that the world could see her lacy thong as she threw her arms around his half-brother's neck. In all of the pictures her clothes barely covered her admittedly remarkable assets, and the camera's glare threw every curve and dip into high-definition exposure.

Remi examined her carefully, searching for weaknesses. His gaze tracked her pert little nose, her wide, sensual mouth, cheekbones sculpted by a master craftsman and a delicate jawline designed to be worshipped with fingers and lips.

The sleek line of her neck dropped to slender, lightly tanned shoulders. Her collarbones were revealed by a sleeveless top, drawing attention to her soft throat and the impressive swell of her breasts. A flat, toned stomach, rounded hips and those endless legs completed the package.

She was flawless. Physically, at least. He had very little doubt that she would be severely lacking in other areas. Except maybe in the—

'Who is she?' he snapped, intensely annoyed with the direction of his thoughts. Who cared how the trollop was in bed?

His mother resumed her seat, her gaze meeting his. 'Her details are on the last page. The rest is still sketchy, but I've seen more than enough to know she presents a potential problem. For one thing, Jules never usually stays in one place more than a few days. He's been in London for almost two weeks. And, unfortunately, these are the least offensive pictures. Whatever is going on between them needs to end. *Now.* The royal transition must be as smooth as possible. So far he's refused my summons for him to return to Montegova. Short of having his bodyguards forcibly put him on a plane—

and risk a kidnapping charge—I have to find a way to bring him to heel.'

Remi's gaze was drawn, against his will, back to the pictures. He flipped to the last page. The woman his half-brother had taken up with was summed up in four lines.

Madeleine Myers
Waitress
Twenty-four years old
College dropout

Distaste filled his mouth. 'You want me to take care of it?' For the sake of his kingdom's reputation, his half-brother's antics needed to be curbed before they attracted unwanted attention.

Queen Isadora linked her fingers and placed them on the desk. 'Jules may not have any interest in behaving like a Montegovan except when it eases his way into casinos and parties, but this cannot be allowed to continue. He pretends otherwise, but he's a little in awe of you. I dare say you scare him a little too. He'll listen to you. And you're the only one I trust to handle this discreetly.' She cleared her throat. 'With the news of my stepping down and your ascension to the throne we can't afford another scandal now. Especially when you announce that you'll be taking a wife at the end of the summer.'

Icy shock gushed through his veins, rendering him speechless for one stunned second. 'I will be *what*?' he demanded when he found his tongue.

'Don't look so shocked. Surely this doesn't come as a surprise? You were all set to do so two years ago.'

Different emotions surged high—a peculiar mingling of pain, futile anger, bitterness and guilt. The first was natural—the pain of a cherished one lost never went away. Although lately the pain had been less and the other emotions more pronounced.

His anger stemmed from a life cut far too short. From all the plans made that would never come to fruition. And the bitterness was aimed squarely at fate and the cruelty of time.

The fact that his fiancée had been on her way to her doctor when the tragedy had struck was irony itself.

Which brought him to the guilt. The culmination of events had been his fault and his alone. For that he had to bear the crushing weight on his soul.

'You would be king and married by now if we hadn't lost Celeste,' his mother said, gentle but firm.

His teeth clenched at the unnecessary reminder. 'I'm well aware of that.' Just as he was well aware that his voice now echoed the chill weaving through his bloodstream. 'But tell me, Mother, where exactly am I to conjure a bride from in three months?'

If he'd hoped to cow her with his caustic tone, he should have known better.

Without missing a beat she opened a tiny drawer directly in front of her chair and took out a single piece of paper. 'The list of candidates we put together for you five years ago is still viable—save for one. She married a count and is already pregnant with her second child.'

The trace of wistfulness in her voice further aggravated Remi, but he kept his emotions on a tight leash, saved his verbal dexterity for the noose caressing his throat.

'I didn't stoop to plucking my future wife from a list

put together by faceless advisers five years ago and I'm not about to do that now.'

Queen Isadora slapped the piece of paper down on the desk. 'Well, that's too bad. This time you don't have the luxury of time or indulgence. Perhaps this is the best way forward. I married for love. You were about to marry the woman of your heart. Look where *that* got us both!'

Remi stiffened. His mother froze in her chair, her eyes widening in shock at her own outburst. Thick silence slammed between them as Remi examined her closer, noted the pallor beneath the make-up, the lines of stress bracketing her eyes.

He'd absorbed more of her duties this past year, but he could still see the strain of office on her face.

Heavy really *was* the head that wore the crown, temporary or not.

A crown that was soon to be placed upon his own head.

Before he could comment she gathered herself with regal poise, her spine ramrod straight as she speared him with a glare.

'Let me be clear, Remirez. I will not sit by and watch all that I've painstakingly rebuilt these past ten years fall to ruin again because your sensibilities won't allow it. You'll go to London, separate your half-brother from this piece of bad news and bring him home. Then you'll pick a bride and announce your betrothal one week before the Solstice Festival. At the festival we'll give an official date for your wedding, which will be three months after your engagement. That gives you six months to get used to the idea of marriage. I'll make myself available to help with preparations if you need me to. Otherwise,

I look forward to being the lucky mother of the groom come September.'

She closed the folder and nudged it an extra inch towards him, before straightening the specially engraved pens which had belonged to his father.

When she was done, she looked him straight in the eye. 'It's time to take your true place as head of this kingdom. I know you won't let me down.'

One minute later, Remi walked out. And, as he'd rightly predicted, everything had changed.

Five more weeks.

Maddie Myers resisted the urge to check her phone for the exact hour and minute before this nightmare was over.

She should never have agreed to this preposterous proposition. So far every second had been hellish.

But then her choices were severely limited. And when a Lamborghini sideswiping you compounded those woes by knocking the grocery shopping paid for with your last tenner out of your hands, you needed to take a moment to accept that things *were* truly awful.

With luck in very limited supply in her world, she'd thanked every star she could name for escaping that horrifying incident with just a few unpleasant-looking bruises, the occasional twinge in her ribs that made it difficult to take a full breath and a sore arm.

To be honest, Maddie was sure it was the shock of being nearly run over that had made her agree to Jules Montagne's scheme in the first place. But by the time she'd downed that second restorative brandy she'd been in the darkest pit of despair, one that not even expensive booze could lift her from. So when the owner of the Lamborghini of Death had offered her a solution to her problems…

Truth be told, at that point she'd been seriously considering the logistics of how to sell one of her kidneys, so a rich assaulter with money to burn had seemed the answer to her prayers.

Nevertheless, it had taken her forty-eight hours to accept his deal. Probably because he'd been cagey about why he needed her in the first place. If Maddie had learned one thing in life, it was to look before she leapt. Blind trust was no longer a flaw that would tarnish her.

She'd trusted her mother to stay and help the family she'd helped break apart. She'd trusted her father every time he'd told her he had his addiction under control. And Greg… He'd been the worst culprit of all.

So when Jules had delivered that stony-faced *ask no questions* ultimatum her first instinct had been to walk out of the fancy wine bar he'd taken her to after nearly running her over, and never look back.

But no matter how many times she'd checked her meagre bank account, or riffled through her belongings in the hope of finding something pawn-worthy, the balance had fallen far too short.

With time running out for her father, she'd had no choice but to return Jules Montagne's phone call.

Of course his help hadn't come for free. Hence her being once again dressed like a high-class escort, listening to him hold court among his circle of trustfundistas and minor royals in another VIP lounge as they guzzled thousands of pounds' worth of champagne.

She'd long since passed the *life is so unfair* and *why me?* stage. And after her mother's shocking desertion Maddie had shrugged off *there's always hope* too.

'Hey, Maddie, smile! The way you're staring into your glass, you'd think somebody's died.'

She plastered on a fake smile while the urge to scream burned through her gullet. True, no one had died. But the man who'd once been a strong, supportive father—a man now sadly broken by his failures—most definitely would, unless she pulled off this performance successfully and collected the payment due to her.

Seventy-five thousand pounds.

The exact amount needed for her father's private kidney operation and aftercare in France.

The exact amount Jules had agreed to pay her if she pretended to be his girlfriend for six weeks.

She raised her gaze from her glass and connected with the gunmetal eyes of her pretend boyfriend. The man who barely spoke to her once they were away from the prying eyes of the paparazzi who dogged his every movement.

'Smile, *cherie*,' he insisted, with a hard, fierce light in his eyes.

She tried again, aiming for authenticity this time. She must have succeeded. He gave a brisk nod and raised his glass to her before swinging back into whatever joke he'd interrupted himself in.

Maddie breathed in relief, winced as her ribs protested, then went back to wondering just how long she could survive down this rabbit hole.

The first time they'd gone out she'd heard one tabloid hack shout a question about Jules's family—specifically how the queen felt about his behaviour. Maddie had asked him about it. He'd shut her down with a snapped response she was sure had been a lie, and reminded her of the *ask no questions* rule.

The possibility that she'd struck a bargain with a minor royal had triggered unease. Media attention was the last thing she wanted.

Despite needing the money desperately, she'd voiced her concerns. Jules's suggestion that she wear headphones with the music turned up high to avoid the paparazzi's questions, and keep her head down to avoid the camera's flash had worked a treat. After all, she couldn't answer questions she couldn't hear.

Maddie was sure that her perceived rudeness had earned her a disparaging label on social media. But the great thing about selling your laptop so you could buy food and using your phone only for emergency calls to avoid expensive bills was the blessed absence of the burden of social media.

So here she was, firmly ensconced in Wonderland, with no inkling of why she was playing pretend girlfriend to a handsome, spoilt, maybe minor royal who travelled with two bodyguards.

She watched him beckon one of them. Jules whispered in his ear, then loudly ordered another half-dozen bottles of Dom Perignon as the young guard headed to the back of the nightclub.

In the gleeful melee that followed the arrival of more booze, very few people noticed Jules following his bodyguard.

The sudden realisation that she'd aligned herself with a man who was headed down the same path of addiction as her father was enough to propel Maddie to her feet. She wasn't sure exactly how she would deal with Jules Montagne if she caught him taking drugs, but her burning anger and anxiety couldn't be contained.

She was halfway across the floor when a commotion by the front doors caught her attention.

Except it wasn't a commotion. It was more a force of nature invading the onyx-and-chrome interior of the Soho nightclub.

Two bodyguards, taller, sharper and burlier than the ones who followed Jules around, parted the crowd.

The man who sauntered forward and paused under a golden spotlight nearly caused Maddie to swallow her tongue.

Frozen in place, she stared unashamedly, certain that the faint tendrils of artificial smoke and strobe lighting were causing her to hallucinate the sheer magnificence of the god-like creature before her.

But no.

He was flesh.

The quiet fury and electric energy blanketing him clearly transmitted through the muscle ticking in his jaw.

He was blood.

Royal blood, if the arrogant, regal authority with which he carried himself and the further four bodyguards who formed a semi-circular barrier around him were any indication.

There was something vaguely familiar about him, although where she could possibly have caught a glimpse before of that square, rugged jaw, those haughty cut-glass cheekbones or those sinfully sensual lips eluded her.

Eyes like polished silver gleamed beneath slashed dark brows, scanning the crowd as he continued to prowl through the semi-dark space.

As he drew closer Maddie knew she should look

away. Not out of shame or discomfort, but out of sheer self-preservation. He radiated enough sensual volatility to urge her to avoid direct eye contact. To take herself out of his magnetising orbit before she was swallowed up in his vortex.

And yet she couldn't make her feet move. In fact she was fairly sure her lungs had stopped working too, now she was witnessing the way he moved. Like a jungle cat on the prowl… Each step a symphony of grace and symmetry and power.

Utterly absorbing.

Infinitely hypnotic.

She was unashamedly gawking when his eyes locked on her. For a fistful of heartbeats he stared.

Hard. Intense. Ice-hot.

Then with long strides he zeroed in on her. His scent invaded her senses as powerfully as the man himself. He smelled of ice and earth, elemental to the core and so utterly unique she could have stood there breathing him in for an eternity, her sore ribs be damned.

'Where is he?' he breathed, and the sound was electrifying enough to send skitters of stinging awareness over her skin.

Whether by some silent command, or simply because everyone in the room knew they were in the presence of greatness, the volume of the music had dropped. That was the reason she heard him and knew that his voice was deep and accented, resulting in sensually wrapped words that triggered a yearning to hear him speak again just for the hell of it.

Maddie knew that would never happen. When this man spoke it was for immediate and masterful effect, no extraneous words necessary.

Seconds passed. His nostrils flared slightly. She realised she hadn't answered.

'I…' She swallowed hard. 'Where is…? Who do you mean?'

'The man you're here with. Jules—'

'What are *you* doing here?'

The snapped question from Jules held anger, panic and defiance, slicing through Maddie's comprehension that the stranger—whoever he was—knew *her*, knew she was with Jules.

He didn't answer immediately. Instead he studied Jules from head to toe, causing him to fidget and adjust his ruffled clothes.

'What did you think would happen when you refused to answer your summons?' he asked icily. 'Did you think your activities would be allowed to continue unchecked?'

Jules opened his mouth, but the other man stopped him with a wave of his elegant hand that would have been poetic had it not been filled with foreboding.

'I will not have this conversation with you here, while you're in this state. Come to my hotel tomorrow morning. We will have breakfast together.'

Each statement was a stern directive, permitting neither disagreement nor disobedience.

It rubbed Jules the wrong way. His chin jutted out. '*Pas possible*. I have plans in the morning.'

Low thunder rumbled across the stranger's face. 'According to your assistant, the only thing you have scheduled is sleeping off your hangover. You will be present, in my suite, at 9:00 a.m. sharp. Is that understood?'

They faced off for less than ten seconds, but it felt like an hour.

Jules's abrupt nod bordered on the insolent, but at the piercing, relentless regard directed towards him his head dropped the way a dog's might when confronted with its disobedience by its master.

The older man stared down at him for another long stretch before his eyes slid sideways to the usually raucous group Jules partied with, who were now respectfully, watchfully silent.

Then his gaze switched to Maddie. He took his time scrutinising her, from the loose knot of her thick hair to the painted toes peeping through her stilettoes.

Every inch of bare skin his gaze touched—and unfortunately there was a lot of it—blazed with an alien, thrilling fire, even the tips of her fingers. She wanted to recoil. Retreat. But there was something weirdly hypnotic about his eyes on her that held her in place, made her struggle to catch even a shallow breath.

Jules followed his line of sight and his eyes widened a touch when he spotted Maddie. Clearly he'd forgotten she existed. He hastily rearranged his expression and reached for her arm. '*Viens, mon amour*, let's go home.'

Maddie stiffened, suppressing another wince.

Even with her limited French, she understood the endearment. In all the time they'd been playing pretence Jules had never called her that. Nor had he invited her to his place. Their routine once they left a club or restaurant and the paparazzi lost interest was for one of his bodyguards to put her in a taxi.

Before she could respond, the stranger shook his head.

'It's 2:00 a.m. You've partied enough for one night. Go home. I'll see to it that Miss Myers makes it to wherever she's going safely.'

Jules's eyes flashed with anger. 'You're assuming she isn't going back to my place. You're assuming she's not my live-in girlfriend.'

'Is she?' Without waiting for an answer he turned sharply to her, silver eyes pinning her to the spot. 'Are you?'

The two words were bullet-sharp.

'That's not the point,' Jules interjected aggressively.

'Either she is or she isn't. Answer the question,' he demanded, without taking his eyes off her.

Very much aware that she had no clue what was going on, Maddie went with the truth. 'No, we're not living together.'

Jules's jaw clenched, but she shrugged it off. If he wanted to give the impression that they were more serious he should have told her. She was uncomfortable enough about the subterfuge as it was.

'Your driver will take you to your hotel, Jules,' the stranger said, glancing pointedly at the hand Jules had on her arm.

Jules muttered a very rude, very French curse. One he intended the man to hear. One that produced a flash of anger in his silver eyes before his expression was ruthlessly blanked.

Without warning Jules yanked her close, cupped the back of her head before slamming his mouth down on hers.

The kiss was over in seconds, but the shocking violation kept Maddie frozen for longer. Stunned, and more than a little incensed, she watched Jules leave without a backward glance, strongly resisting the urge to swipe her hand across her mouth.

She knew he'd kissed her for effect, to annoy the

domineering man standing before her, whose gaze was now a darker silver as it swept over cheeks gone pale before returning to her mouth. And she knew, despite the burning urge to rub off the last trace of that kiss, it would be a dead giveaway that might cost her a lot in the long run.

So she raised her chin, met eyes that blazed with a fierce light she couldn't fathom.

'Come,' he said abruptly. Then, like Jules, he turned and walked out.

Maddie shook her head once to clear it. When nothing altered the sensation of having just experienced a furious electric storm, she stumbled back on shaky legs to her seat.

She had no intention of following that arrogant, dangerously compelling man anywhere. The only place she was headed was home, to the flat she shared with her father. To the safety and discomfort of her single bed.

Excited chatter and camera phones aimed her way hastened her movements. She still had no clear idea what had transpired a few minutes ago, but she wasn't sticking around to be the cynosure of all eyes.

She'd have enough to deal with come morning anyway. For one, she had to ensure her father got through another day without succumbing to the addiction that had decimated not just *his* life but the relatively care-free family life she'd taken for granted.

She pushed harrowing thoughts of her father's addiction and her mother's desertion aside, stood up—and was met with a wall of muscle.

'Miss? Come with me, please.'

It was one of the superior bodyguards. Far from assuming the stranger had accepted she had no intention of following, he'd left a minder behind to ensure she obeyed his command.

The chatter was rising. Curious looks and pointing fingers were aimed at her as she scrambled to find a way around her dilemma.

Stay here and deal with the gossip-hungry pack, or go outside and deal with the even more dangerous predator who had made every nerve in her body zing to life?

'Oh, my God, did you actually see him?'

'He's like...a god!'

'I could actually drop dead from how drop-dead gorgeous he is!'

'Who is she, *anyway?'*

That last question propelled her feet forward, fuelled by the distinct impression that the bodyguard wasn't above physically bundling her up and delivering her to his master.

Outside, the sleekest, shiniest black limousine idled at the kerb. The shiver that lanced through her when she spotted it had nothing to do with the chilled late-March air.

As she drew closer the driver, standing to attention, swung the back door open.

The interior light was off, so all Maddie saw with the aid of the streetlights were long, trouser-clad masculine legs and polished shoes.

'Get in, Miss Myers.' The instruction was deep, resolute and throbbed with impatience.

She was a few dozen yards from Soho's bustling main street. Her legs were strong enough to outrun the bodyguards...

'Take my advice and don't bother.' The suggestion was an arrogant drawl, wrapped in steel.

With every fibre of her being Maddie wanted to refuse. But she knew it would be futile. Whoever he was, unmistakable power and authority oozed from him. Plus, his bodyguards were in prime condition.

So, with a snatched breath, she climbed in. The earlier she got this over and done with, the quicker she could go home, she told herself. She needed to be at work in a few short hours.

The moment she slid into the car, the door shut behind her.

For tense seconds she withstood those eerie eyes glinting at her, withstood the need to glance at him and pretended interest in the luxury interior and the long, soft leather bench seat. But inevitably her gaze was drawn to him, like an unwitting moth to a flame. Again his gaze dropped to her mouth before rising to meet hers, leaving her shaky and tingling all over again.

Enough of this.

'Who are you and how do you know who I am?' she demanded, when it became clear he was just going to stare at her with those electric eyes.

The question seemed to startle him. Then his head went back in a manner that could only be termed *exceptionally regal*.

'My name is Remirez Alexander Montegova, Crown Prince of the Kingdom of Montegova. I know who you are because I have an excellent team of private investigators who make it their job to furnish me with that kind of information. Now you will tell *me* how much it will take for you walk away from my brother.'

CHAPTER TWO

'*Your brother?*' Maddie cringed at the squeak in her voice.

'Technically, half-brother. We share the same father.' His voice was coated in dark ice.

She shook her head, confused. 'But…but his name is Jules Montagne. And he's French.'

Whereas this man's accent was an enthralling mix of Italian, French and Spanish.

Crown Prince Remirez…*oh, my God*…shrugged one rugged shoulder. 'He's French on his mother's side. And the name he uses is a ruse, I suspect, to throw people off the scent.'

'Off the scent of what?' she asked, grappling with the alarming disclosure and the fact that everything about the man lounging like a resting panther finally made sense. As did the fact that the resemblance she'd noted was to Jules.

He remained silent, then a tiny interior light was illuminated above his head. Once again he was bathed in golden light. He seemed even larger against the dark backdrop of the car, his jet-black hair glinting, the shoulders beneath his bespoke suit broader and even more imposing.

'Off the scent of his true identity. Off the scent of gold-diggers, con artists and hangers-on,' he replied with icy-cold condemnation.

There was little doubt the accusation was aimed at her. And it deeply irked Maddie that even that couldn't stop her body's hyper-awareness of him. Couldn't stop her noticing her clammy hands or the elevated temperature between her thighs.

'Right. I see.'

'I'm sure you do,' he replied wryly.

She leaned closer to the window and flinched as her arm protested. She dragged her gaze from the view of Waterloo Bridge. 'Where are you taking me?'

'Where I said I would deliver you. To your home,' he answered simply. 'What's wrong with your arm?'

'Excuse me?'

His gaze dropped.

She followed it and realised she was rubbing her lower arm. She hastily dropped her hand. 'Nothing. I'm fine. You know where I live?'

His gaze stayed on her arm for another handful of seconds before he replied, 'Yes. I also know where you work, where you went to school and who your dentist is.'

Apprehension fizzled inside her. 'Is that some sort of threat?'

'I've merely armed myself with knowledge. After all, it is power, is it not? Did you not get into this car to do the same?'

'I got into this car because you sent your supersized bodyguard after me.'

'He didn't touch you.' The finality behind the words indicated she hadn't been touched because he'd wished it to be so.

She forced a laugh, despite the surge of energy thrumming through her belly. 'Oh, wow, I'll consider myself lucky, then.'

He knew everything about her. Did he know about her father? Her mother? Greg? Was he aware of the shameful secret that dogged her every wakeful moment and followed her into her nightmares?

'You haven't answered my question,' he said.

She swallowed the pulse of anger in her throat. 'And I'm not going to. It's insulting. I don't know you from Adam and yet you think you can just throw money at me and I'll do your bidding?'

He didn't respond immediately. Not until the limo stopped at a set of traffic lights a mile from her flat. 'I haven't done any throwing since you haven't given me your price. How long have you known Jules?'

Unease ramped up the vibrations in her belly. 'I don't see how that's relevant—'

'You've known him a little over a week. You've been out with him almost every night and yet you've never returned to his apartment with him.'

The depth of his knowledge sent a sheet of ice gliding over her skin. 'That doesn't mean anything.'

'On the contrary, that leads me to conclude you're holding out for something. What is it, Miss Myers?'

She smiled. 'Sex, drugs and rock and roll—what else?'

Her dripping sarcasm went straight over his head as he threw a disdainful glance out of the window.

'Jules wouldn't be caught dead in this neighbourhood. So, unless you've been copulating somewhere other than his apartment, I highly doubt it's sex. And I know for a fact that it's not drugs.'

'That's ridiculous. How would you know that?' she threw back.

Slightly narrowed eyes were the only indication that he found her questioning insolent. 'Because it's a condition of his remaining in my royal bursar's good graces that he stays clean. In return for his generous allowance, he's tested for drugs on a regular basis.'

Although the information allayed her earlier fears, Maddie was still disturbed by the revelations. 'Tested? You're saying that you *pay* him to stay off drugs?'

Prince Remirez's lashes swept down. 'Among many other things,' he murmured.

Curiosity ramped high. 'Really? Like what?' she asked, telling herself it really was time she found out more about the man who'd promised to pay her to pretend to be his girlfriend.

'Like things that are none of your concern,' Prince Remirez returned chillingly. 'And, just in case you're inclined to peddle what I've just told you, know that I'll sue you for everything you own if any of this makes it into tomorrow's papers.'

'Yeah, good luck with that,' she replied waspishly, before she could help herself.

'You think my caution is idle?' he mused coolly, his stance relaxed in a way that said he found her in no way threatening.

She shook her head, smiling with more than a little relief when the limo pulled into her street.

'Not at all. I meant good luck finding anything of value to sue me for.'

The moment the words left her lips she wanted to snatch them back. But it was too late.

Eyes like laser beams latched onto the truth. 'You're destitute,' he declared after a taut pause.

Shame crawled over Maddie's skin. Followed instantaneously by searing anger. 'What I am is none of your business. We're strangers to one another. So *I* won't jump to the conclusion that you're a rich, pompous royal bastard who looks down his aristocratic nose at the less fortunate, if *you* don't assume I'm some worthless gold-digger who's just itching to jump straight out of your car and into a paparazzo's pocket.'

'I don't have proof that you're a worthless gold-digger, but I'm growing certain that you're a shameless exhibitionist,' he replied in that charismatically accented voice that threw her for a second before his meaning sank in.

'*Excuse me?* What gives you the right—?' She glanced down sharply and gasped as flames of embarrassment shot into her face.

Oh, God.

The hem of her dress had crept up almost to her crotch, and somehow one creamy slope of a breast was exposed in the gaping neckline of her halter top. The wardrobe Jules had provided for their outings was one of the many things she'd baulked at. One of the many things he'd stated were deal-breakers.

'I suggest you pull yourself together before that notion becomes concrete,' he advised, with a new husk in his voice and a banked blaze in his eyes that directed the flamed inward, singeing low in her belly and then lower, in places she didn't want to acknowledge.

She hurriedly pulled down her hem and adjusted her neckline, aware that his gaze tracked her every movement. Aware she'd been judged and found severely lacking.

When she was as adequately covered as she could be, she fixed her eyes on the door handle. 'Are we done here?'

He sat back, master of everything he surveyed—which eerily felt as if it included her—and crossed one leg over the other. 'That depends,' he drawled.

'On what?' she asked, still unable to look him in the eye.

He didn't respond.

More than a little unnerved at the racing of her heart, she lifted her gaze to his. 'On *what*?' she repeated.

A slow, predatory smile lifted the corners of his lips. Beneath the light his eyes gleamed, taking on an unnerving, hypnotising colour that made her believe he could see right to the heart of her. To the sensual vibrations stroking her nerve-endings. To the unsettling licks of fire in her belly.

Her fingers tightened around her bag, and she was about to demand he answer her when he gave a brisk nod to someone out of sight. The door immediately sprang open.

'You'll find out in due course. Goodnight, Miss Myers.'

Maddie's nights since she had been forced to abandon her child psychology courses at university and return home to care for her father had been plagued with worrying about finding a way to keep the roof over their heads and her father from the pit of addiction. Sleeplessness had become the norm, the creaking of the cheap slats beneath her mattress the discordant accompaniment to her anxiety.

Tonight, however, other thoughts and images reeled through her mind, and agitation drove her fingers into her worn duvet as a plethora of emotions eroded any hope of sleep.

Disbelief—she'd met a true-life, drop-dead gorgeous crown prince who might have stepped off the silver screen.

Anger—he'd blatantly stated that he was threatening her because he suspected she was after something from his brother. Technically true, but still…

Arousal? No, she wasn't going to touch that.

And anxiety—*'You will find out in due course.'*

Did he mean the agreement she'd made with Jules? If so, how?

It was clear he held a great deal of sway over his younger half-brother, despite Jules's defiant attitude. Would he stoop to denying her what Jules had promised her?

That last thought kept her awake for the rest of the night until, giving up on sleep, she dragged herself out of bed just before her alarm went off at six.

Her father was already up, although not dressed, when she reached the kitchen. Maddie paused in the doorway, breath held, and examined him. His gauntness was even more pronounced than it had been a month ago—the result of his failing kidneys on top of the strong painkillers he'd become addicted to when his thriving property business had failed in the crash a decade ago.

He'd hidden his addiction for years, in a misguided attempt to keep up appearances and hang on to a wife who had made no bones about the fact that she expected to live a certain lifestyle and demanded her husband provide it.

A near overdose had brought everything to light three years ago, showing the shocking damage Henry Myers had done to his body. It had also been the start of many promises to get clean that had resulted time and again in relapse, and the raiding of their meagre finances to seek help for him that had pulled them deeper into destitution.

Eventually the fall from affluent lifestyle to nursing an addict in a tiny flat in one of the poorest neighbourhoods in London had become too much for her mother.

Once upon a time her father had been healthy, outgoing, a pillar of a man his peers had looked up to. Maddie's childhood had been pampered and carefree, if a little emotionally unrewarding. She'd learned not to complain early on, when she'd realised her father loved her but was always busy and her mother was more preoccupied with retail therapy than her daughter's emotional well-being. Even when the distance between her and her mother had widened, Maddie had been secure in her father's abstract affection.

All of that had ended with Priscilla Myers's three-minute phone call to Maddie at university. She'd had enough. Maddie needed to come home and take care of her father because she wasn't prepared to live in poverty and disgrace. Any guilt about abandoning the husband she'd promised to stand by in sickness and in health hadn't been reflected in her voice. She'd walked away without a backward glance or a forwarding address.

Maddie bottled up the still ravaging anguish now as she fully entered the kitchen. 'You're up early.' She kept her voice light and airy.

Her father shrugged half-heartedly. 'Couldn't sleep,' he muttered.

'Do you want breakfast? Toast and tea?' she asked hopefully.

He shook his head. 'I'm not hungry. Maybe later.'

He was avoiding her gaze—a sure sign that the demons of addiction were snapping at his heels again. Her heart dropped. Had she owned more than the couple of hundred pounds she kept for emergencies in her bank account she would have taken the day off and stayed home to offer the support he baulked at but clearly needed.

Pushing back the despair, she pinned a smile on her face. 'Mrs Jennings will look in on you later. She'll fix you lunch if you're hungry. There's food in the fridge.'

His mouth compressed but he didn't reply. Maddie pushed past the bite of guilt. Although her father suspected it, she hadn't confirmed that desperation had driven her to pay their next-door neighbour a small sum to look in on him a few times a day.

After he had been bumped from the transplant list twice after relapsing, she'd resorted to desperate ways of keeping an eye on him. The last barrage of tests had revealed he was weeks away from full renal failure.

The doctors had advised that they wouldn't sanction her father's operation unless he remained clean for at least six months. He'd waved away her worries when she'd talked to him about it but so far he'd stayed clean.

All she needed to do was come through with the funds required for his operation. Funds entirely dependent on whether she finished her stint with Jules Montagne. Correction: Jules Montegova. Half-brother to Crown Prince Remirez Alexander Montegova.

The latter's image rose up, large and imposing, dragging a small shiver down her spine as she finished her breakfast.

By the time she was done with the morning rush hour customers at the café where she worked near Oxford Street, the seed of worry that had taken root in the small hours had grown into a bramble bush.

Jules normally sent her a text in the early hours before he went to bed, telling her where and when to meet for their next 'date'. When midday came and went without a word from him, her worry escalated to full-blown anxiety.

She didn't want to waste her precious phone minutes calling him, but the inkling that something was wrong wouldn't ease. Too much hinged on finishing what she'd started with Jules for her to prevaricate about this. She decided she would call him during her break.

The café was quieter, but still half full. Besides her, two other waitresses were busy delivering dishes to customers, with a third, Di, cleaning the table next to where Maddie was sorting cutlery.

'Holy cow, it's Prince Remirez!' Di screeched.

Maddie almost jumped out of her skin, nearly dropping the two dozen forks in her hands. 'What?'

Di pointed, wide-eyed, at the window.

Heart slamming against her ribs, Maddie turned and watched the man she'd spent far too many precious hours thinking about examining the café sign and the pavement with the same dripping disdain he'd shown for her neighbourhood last night.

The late March sun burst through the clouds in that moment, outlining his upturned haughty face in jaw-dropping relief.

Last night, in the dark nightclub and darker limo, she'd thought his breathtaking male beauty too good to be true. Now, with the sun caressing every spectacular feature, Maddie was left in no doubt that from head to toe the man next in line to the throne of Montegova was a magnificent male specimen.

She managed to drag her gaze from that rugged jaw and captivating face long enough to glance at her colleague. 'You know who he is?'

Di rolled her eyes. '*Duh!* Every female with a pulse over the age of fourteen knows who he is. His brother Zak is equally hot. I wonder what the Crown Prince is doing here, though. I would've thought Bond Street was more his speed if he's shopping. Hey, don't royals have minions to do that sort of—? *Oh, my God*, he's coming in *here*!'

Maddie turned away, praying Di was wrong. He wasn't here for her. *He couldn't be.* In the dark of a nightclub, in the midst of minor celebrities and royalty, it was easy to explain away a crown prince's fleeting interest in her—even to herself.

Here, among the cheap plastic furniture and even cheaper food of a street corner café, it was difficult to rationalise why *the hottest man alive* would seek her out.

But what were the chances that he was here on some other mission?

Di continued to chatter away. Maddie kept her back to the door, despite the mocking voice that said she was burying her head in the sand.

Moments later she heard the hush in the café, heard the firm, confident footfalls of a man who believed he owned the very ground he walked on—right before she felt the mildly earth-shaking vibrations of his presence behind her.

'Miss Myers.'

Dear God, she hadn't imagined the impact of that

voice. Nor had she imagined its pulse-destroying effect on her.

She tried fruitlessly to fight the shivers coursing through her as she turned around. And promptly lost her grip on the forks in her hand.

The clatter was astounding.

Face flaming, Maddie dropped to her knees, furiously scrambling for the forks. Before her, a pair of polished hand-stitched shoes remained planted. Unmoving. She refused to look up, refused to acknowledge the existence of the man clad in an expensive, dark navy pinstriped suit that probably cost more than her year's salary. She crawled around him, snatching up the utensils as her face grew hotter. When she had them all she sat back on her heels, prepared to rise.

'Miss Myers?'

Maddie bit her lip, knowing she couldn't avoid looking at him. She tilted her head, her breath strangling all over again when her eyes clashed with his silver-grey ones. They were ferociously intense, even as one eyebrow slowly lifted mockingly and he examined her flushed face.

'Um...yes?' She was sure embarrassment was what had rendered her voice a husky mess, *not* the charged volts shooting through her pelvis and the stinging awareness that she was at eye level with his crotch.

She blinked, her brain emptying of everything but one single, breath-stealing erotic image.

'You missed one.'

A throat cleared. Hastily she glanced down, saw one cheap scratched fork held between his long, neatly tapered fingers.

She snatched it from him. 'Thank you.'

Still on her knees, she placed the forks on the nearest table, then froze when Prince Remirez extended one elegant hand towards her.

Her heart leapt into her throat as she considered the many ways she could refuse his assistance without causing offence.

There were none.

So she placed her hand in his, felt his fingers glide across her palm on their way to gripping hers. She'd once read a novel in which the heroine described feeling pure electricity when she touched the man of her dreams. Maddie had rolled her eyes then.

Now she sent a silent apology to the maligned character.

Crown Prince Remirez would never be the man of her dreams, and she wasn't going to waste her time counting the many ways why, but the reality that singed and branded and claimed that small portion of her body promised that she would never shake another hand without remembering this captivating moment.

Her insides liquefied as he tightened his grip and tugged her to her feet. The slight tautening of his face and the flare in his eyes told her he wasn't completely unaffected by what was happening. Nor did he miss her wince as her arm twinged in pain.

The moment she felt steady on her feet she tried to snatch her hand from his. He kept hold of her for a moment longer before he released her.

When she could breathe again Maddie threw a furtive glance around her. As suspected, every single gaze in the café was fixed on her, including her boss's—although his curiosity was beginning to dissolve into annoyance.

'Would…would you like a table, um… Your High-ness?' Was that the correct form of address? Or was it Your Grace? 'You can pick any one you like. I'll be with you as soon as I finish putting—'

'I'm not here to dine, Miss Myers.' He cut across her, not bothering to keep his voice down. Or the disdain out of it.

She reminded herself that she needed this job and therefore couldn't afford to be rude to patrons or non-patrons. 'In that case I can't really help you, since I'm working. Maybe we can—'

'It's in your interest to make time. Now.'

About to refuse, because her heart rate didn't seem interested in slowing down, and because he really was a little too potent to her senses, she paused. Something in his voice warned her against it.

Belatedly she remembered that he'd summoned Jules to breakfast this morning. Had Jules divulged their con-nection? Was that why he was here?

She searched his face and came away with nothing but further evidence of his heart-stopping gorgeous-ness.

A quick glance at the clock showed it was a quarter past eleven. The lunchtime rush hour wouldn't start for another half hour. 'Jim, can I take my break now? I'll make it up later.'

The head chef, who also happened to be the café's owner, glanced from her to Prince Remirez and then, barely hiding his irritation, nodded. 'I s'pose so.'

She flashed him a grateful smile, then dived into the small cubicle that doubled up as a changing and break room to get her bag. Slinging it crossways over her shoulder, she hurried through the café and out onto the pavement.

Where a small crowd had gathered, their camera phones ready to capture the image of the most captivating man on earth.

'We'll have more privacy in the car,' Prince Remirez pronounced smoothly, a second before his hand arrived at her waist and nudged her firmly in the direction of the open back door of a limo.

Maddie entered, immediately noting the different configuration of the seats from last night's car. There was no bench seat on the far side behind the driver. Which left her no choice but shuffle along the seat as Prince Remirez slid in after her.

The door shut behind him and instantly the atmosphere closed in around them. The push of air wrapped his scent around her, triggering that insane urge to bury her face in his neck and drown herself in his scent.

Whether it came from a bottle or it was a specially branded scent, it was lethal enough to be seriously addictive to women.

Addictive.

The word brought her up short, flinging her foolish ruminations into harsh reality. 'Okay, Your Highness. You have fifteen minutes.'

He adjusted his cuffs, rested his elegant hands on his thighs before fixing his ferocious eyes on her. 'Your business with Jules is over,' he stated bluntly.

Maddie tried not to panic, but fear raced up her spine and threatened to paralyse her all the same.

After forcing herself to take a few slow, rib-bruising breaths, she pulled her phone from her pocket. 'With all due respect, I want to hear it from him.'

Prince Remirez glanced at her phone. 'He's already on a plane to Montegova. You won't see him or talk to him again. Your number has been blocked from his phone permanently so save yourself the trouble.'

A cold shiver ploughed through her. 'Why are you doing this?'

He reached into his breast pocket and extracted a dark burgundy card with sleek gold numbers embossed on the front and back. 'I came here to tell you that if you wish to salvage anything from this I am prepared to hear you out.' He nodded at the card. 'My address and private number are on the back. You have twenty-four hours to use it. Then I too will be out of your reach.'

CHAPTER THREE

LAST NIGHT, SEEING her in real life for the first time, Remi had thought her beauty exceptional.

Right now, watching the muted light from the sunroof bathe her in a soft glow, she was even more exquisite.

Maddie Myers's beauty was like nothing he'd ever seen. For starters, he couldn't put his finger on why she would look so magnificent in a cheap, drab waitress's uniform when last night she'd been dressed in finer, albeit more risqué, attire.

The other puzzling thing was that Remi had dated women who were equally beautiful. And yet something about this woman, whose beauty oozed from her very pores, triggered a stark, cloying hunger within him that he hadn't quite been able to get a handle on.

That hunger had roared to life the moment he'd walked into that dismal café, and intensified when she'd dropped to her knees before him. Even now base images reeled through his mind. Images he had no business accommodating in public.

Years spent perfecting the art of schooling his expression had saved him from blatantly telegraphing his reaction. But those images were etched clearly in his brain, gaining lurid purchase as her plump lips part in shock.

'Jules is really gone?' she demanded huskily.

Remi gritted his teeth, finding the chore of discussing his half-brother with this woman intensely unsatisfactory. 'Yes.'

Brows two shades darker than her honey-gold hair bunched together in confusion. 'But… I don't understand.'

'What's there to understand? He's finally decided to grow up and make a meaningful contribution to the kingdom.'

'Just like that?' she asked sceptically.

'Of course not. It's taken a considerable amount of time to make him accept his responsibilities.'

'And you came here to get him to do that?'

Remi shrugged. 'It was past time someone did.' He watched her carefully for signs that whatever had been going on between her and Jules was more than a light dalliance.

Her eyelashes swept down, shielding her expression from him. He fisted his hand on his thigh to curb the urge to cup her chin and expose her gaze to him.

After a moment, she swiped the tip of her tongue over her bottom lip. 'Did he…did he say anything about me?' she enquired gruffly.

His irritation grew. 'Should he have?'

Her long lashes flew up, jade-green eyes flashing at him before she turned to stare blindly out of the window.

Remi continued to study her. Although her fingers twisted the handle of her bag in agitation, her expression didn't reflect the forlorn anguish of a discarded lover.

No, Maddie Myers's demeanour betrayed a different sort of torment. One of panicked frustration.

Jules had been an important cog in the wheel of her plans. A thwarted plan she was now furiously re-assessing.

Still, he needed to be sure. 'You didn't kiss him back.'

Her head whipped towards him, her eyes widening. 'What?'

'Last night your supposed lover kissed you goodnight. You didn't kiss him back. In fact you seemed disturbingly apathetic.'

Remi was certain that had been one of the reasons he hadn't acted on his visceral need to separate them. The other had been because he hadn't wanted to attract even more attention than his presence in that seedy nightclub had already garnered.

Maddie Myers schooled her features in a way that would have made his childhood deportment instructors proud. 'Didn't I? You must be mistaken.'

'I was not. Why were you with Jules?' The question was beginning to grate, like a tiny stone in his shoe.

'According to you, he's several thousand miles away. Therefore why we were together no longer matters, does it?'

Her gaze dropped to her phone, and there was a contemplative look in her eyes.

'It matters if you're planning to contact him the moment you're out of my sight. If you are, I seriously advise against it.'

Defiant eyes met his. 'I fail to see how you're going to stop me, since the minute I step out of this vehicle I intend never to see you again.'

'You delude yourself if you think you'll be free of me that easily.'

'And you delude *your*self with...with whatever you think this interrogation is. I owe you nothing. Getting into this car with you was a courtesy. One you've outworn. So, if you'll excuse me, I'm going back to work now before I annoy my boss.'

She reached for the handle to the door that would open onto the street.

He darted forward and seized her wrist, quiet fury laced with something that felt alarmingly close to dread fizzing through his bloodstream. 'Are you always this careless with your safety?' he demanded, aware his voice was harsh and gruff.

He told himself it had nothing to do with the guilt fused into his being. Or the breathtaking smoothness of the skin stretched over her racing pulse.

For some reason she found his question amusing, although her thousand-watt smile barely made an appearance before it was extinguished again. 'Did you not ask your brother how we met?'

All he'd wanted from Jules this morning was his agreement to board the royal plane back to Montegova, and a promise that he would cease contact with Maddie Myers immediately. Discussions of duty and responsibility had been shelved when he'd realised his brother was severely hungover.

'The subject didn't come up.'

'Well, he nearly ran me over with his supercar. And, no, I wasn't being reckless. The signal to cross was still green when he hit me.'

Remi's blood went deathly cold. Over the last two years he'd lived with an unending torrent of might-havebeens. All the things he might have done to alter events. The image of Maddie Myers lying lifeless on a filthy pavement awoke demons he'd fought hard and failed to conquer.

'Jules hit you with his car?' He was aware his voice was a thin, icy blade. But it was only when she flinched that his gaze dropped to the hold he had on her.

He loosened his grip as other things began to fall into place. The wincing she tried to hide. The flash of pain across her face last night in the car and when he'd touched her in the café.

Rage rose to mingle with the guilt. 'How badly were you hurt?' The gravel-rough demand seared his throat.

Her head dipped and her gaze fell to her lap. 'Besides my pride and a few bruises and scratches, I'd say the groceries that met their end on Camberwell New Road came off worse.'

Ice-cold fingers gripped his nape. 'Don't be flippant about it.'

His harsh rebuttal made her flinch. When her eyes darted to his fists, Remi realised he'd clenched them so hard the knuckles were bloodless.

'I… It wasn't a big deal,' she whispered.

He slowly unfurled his hands. Sucked in one long breath. 'Was that when you struck this secret bargain between the two of you?'

A flash of alarm crossed her face, then evaporated to leave faint pink spots on her cheeks. Without answering she turned resolutely to the door. 'This conversation is over. Goodbye, Your Highness.'

Remi had no intention of letting her get away. Not until he'd delved into these new revelations. Revelations that had him secretly reeling.

'I've changed my mind. You no longer have twenty-four hours.'

He picked up the card she'd dropped on the seat between them and slid it back into his pocket.

He nodded abruptly. And a moment later his car had left the kerb and the café behind.

Her shocked gaze swung to the window, then back to him. 'What the hell do you think you're doing?'

'We're going to talk. In one hour you'll either have decided you don't work at that café any more or your boss will be adequately compensated for your absence and you can return to work tomorrow morning. Either way, neither of you will lose. Put your seatbelt on.'

'No! I don't know how things work in your country, but here what you're doing is called kidnapping!'

Remi caught her arm just beneath the short sleeve of her cheap shirt, again noting the satin-smoothness of her skin and the sizzle of miniature fireworks that transmitted from her skin to his.

Back in the café, when he'd first touched her, he mocked himself for over-exaggerating the sensation. Now he knew for sure as the blood heated in his veins.

Her breath hitched and her alluring eyes dropped to where he held her before she jerked away from him. 'Please don't touch me.'

Reluctantly, he released her. She gave a tiny shake of her head, as if she found the sizzling, unwanted chemistry as confounding as he did. That knowledge only intensified the urgency rampaging through him.

'You will tell me why you're anxious to get in touch with Jules. After you tell me in detail about your first meeting.' He frowned as his memory came up blank on that part of Maddie Myers's recent history. 'Why isn't there a record of the accident or a hospital visit?'

Sparks flared in her eyes. 'Because there wasn't one. And in case I didn't get around to mentioning it last night, it's loathsome of you to pry into my life the way you blithely believe you have a right to.'

'Why wasn't there one?' he demanded.

'Because your brother didn't take me to hospital, that's why.'

This time he couldn't contain his curse, the fury that tripled his heartbeat or the churning alarm that underpinned all his emotions. 'He nearly ran you over and you didn't demand to be taken to a hospital?'

Her expression closed and she avoided his gaze. 'I told you—'

'You're trying to hide the fact that you're favouring your right arm and yet you flinch and grow pale with every contact. Either you're truly intent on deluding yourself that your injury is no big deal...' he paused as a deeper bolt of emotion, a protectiveness he didn't welcome, kicked him in the gut '...or there's another reason you're burying your head in the sand.'

He hit the intercom and instructed his driver on a different destination.

'Either way, it has nothing to do with you,' she replied stiffly.

'That's where you're wrong, Miss Myers.'

Wary eyes blinked at him. 'What's that supposed to mean?'

'It means it's my duty to ensure that nothing a member of my family does comes back to bite us when we least expect it. And now I have a better idea of what went on between you and Jules we can get down to the bottom line. But not until I find out what I'm dealing with.'

'I… I don't understand.'

'I'm taking you to the hospital, Madeleine. You can protest if you wish, but know this: the earlier you deal with me, the earlier we can be rid of each other.' He waited a beat, despite the volatile emotions churning through his bloodstream. 'So will you come with me of your own free will?'

Green eyes flew to his and again he caught the faint alarm in the bronze-flecked depths. Her lightly glossed lips parted and she sucked in a slow breath. After a moment, she nodded. 'Yes.'

The churning subsided a touch. 'Good.'

Reaching over her shoulder, he drew the seat belt across her body, forcing his gaze not to linger on her breasts as he secured her in place.

'This isn't a hospital! This is—'

'My private physician.'

'At a private clinic in Harley Street?'

Remi frowned at the accusation. 'Other than pointing out the geographical location, do you have a point?'

'Yes. I have a point. I can't afford a private doctor.'

Agitation charged her movements and he caught her wince as she freed herself from the seatbelt.

'*Dio*, calm down before you aggravate your injury.'

'First of all, we don't even know if I *have* an injury. Secondly, please stop ordering me about.'

He took a sustaining breath and reminded himself why he was doing this. For his family.

For reasons he intended to get to the bottom of before the day was out, neither Jules nor his bodyguards had seen fit to report the incident with Maddie. Remi shuddered to imagine what the press would do if it got out.

He wasn't out of the woods yet. He needed to play this right to prevent any possibility of a scandal further down the line.

But beyond that he knew there was another reason. The unquenchable need to make sure history didn't repeat itself. That he didn't spend more nights racked with guilt about someone else—even if that person was this stunningly gorgeous but aggravating blonde who looked nothing like his Celeste but who nevertheless evoked astounding, groin-stirring sensations within him.

He ruthlessly pushed the hot throb of lust aside and nodded to his driver to open the door. 'I value my time and my privacy. I'm assured of both here. And you insult me by suggesting that I would expect you to pay for medical attention necessitated through my brother's actions. Now, do you have any further objections?'

Plump lips he found far too tempting stayed shut for a long moment before she exited the vehicle. He followed, telling himself the tingle in his fingers *wasn't* from the desire to touch her again, to place his hand on that delicate waist and guide her into the clinic.

In fact, he made sure to keep his distance from her as they were checked in and Maddie was escorted into a suite where a barrage of scans were lined up.

Fifty minutes later he stared out of the window, jaw clenched, as they were driven away from Harley Street towards his hotel.

'You pushed for those tests and now you're not going to say anything?' Maddie asked testily from beside him.

He kept his gaze on the passing view. He deemed it much safer, because something about the sling around

Maddie's arm agitated his every last demon and fired a level of fury he'd never known before.

'A hairline fracture on your ulna. Two more on your ribs. Bone-deep bruises on your left hip that will take two more weeks to heal.' The words fell from his lips like shards of glass.

'I know what the doctor said. I was there too, re-member?'

He rounded on her, knowing his rage was misguided but unable to stop himself nevertheless. He speared his fingers in her hair, ignoring her hot gasp as he dropped his face to hers.

'I don't know who I'm more furious at—you for not insisting on seeing a doctor or Jules for being a blind, selfish idiot and landing me in this situation,' he breathed against her mouth.

She gasped, and the sound transmitted straight to the core of his roiling emotions. To her credit she said nothing, for once choosing the wise course. But her silence meant that other sensations rose to the fore—her closeness, her unsteady breathing, the warmth of her delicate jaw beneath his fingers, the wild pulse racing at her throat. The velvety smoothness of her lips.

Against his better judgement he glided his thumb over her lower lip, then suppressed a thick groan as her lips parted.

The gentle rocking of the car jerked him to his senses. Just as shame and guilt slammed into him.

Celeste.

Every moment in this woman's presence, behaving like a base animal, betrayed his late fiancée's memory. And dragged him deeper into a quagmire he was be-ginning to fear he would never be free of.

* * *

The top floor of the Four Seasons hotel was on perma-
nent reservation to the Montegovan royal family since
they were frequent visitors to England. And perhaps
its most valued asset was the discreet private access it
granted to its VIP guests.

Remi was grateful for the entrance now, not only
because it shielded him from prying eyes, but also because it was secure enough not to require his bodyguards' presence.

He didn't need witnesses to his agitated state, nor
did he need indiscreet enquiries as to why he was es-
corting a woman wearing a waitress's uniform and a
sling to his suite.

A gorgeous, dangerous woman with lips as soft as silk.

He shoved his balled fists into his pockets, cursing
his libido's atrocious timing and the instrument respon-
sible for its reawakening.

Despite the revelations of the last two hours, he
hadn't changed his initial assessment of Madeleine
Myers. A typical gold-digger out to capitalise on an
unfortunate incident. Except now she had a solid basis
from where to launch her attack.

His mind froze as the horror of it replayed itself. *Dio*,
Jules had nearly run her over. Had she been petrified?
Or had shock numbed her?

Unbidden, the stark script of Celeste's last few days
tumbled through his mind, reminding him of life's fra-
gility with a punch in the gut.

He sucked in a deep breath and slowly loosened
his fists. The circumstances of his fiancée's death and
Maddie's accident were miles apart. Yet that underlying
helplessness against fate remained.

'Has no one ever told you it's rude to stare so openly?' she demanded waspishly as the lift arrived.

His gaze flickered over her brazenly defiant face. 'Not if they risked a flogging, no,' he answered drolly, and silently cursed Jules again.

But it wasn't his brother's fault he was caught in the loop of his past. The conversation in his mother's office had also raked up a subject he didn't want to think about, never mind act on it.

Nonetheless it was an issue he needed to tackle.

He gestured Maddie forward. With another wary glance at him she preceded him into the lift that would take them directly to his penthouse suite.

When they exited, seconds later, she surprised him by neither glancing around at the luxurious decor or at the priceless Montegovan paintings and artefacts that lined the hallway. Without fail, every visitor granted access to this private floor was bowled over by the opulence and grandeur his mother had spared no expense in commissioning five years ago.

Still, Remi didn't doubt Maddie Myers's motives for one minute. She was definitely after something. And he was determined to find out what.

The moment they entered the suite, she faced him across the space of the vast living room. 'I'm here now. Can we get this over with so I can return to my life?'

'Is that what you'll do once you leave here? Return to your life and forget all about Jules and my family?'

She frowned. 'Of course. What else do you think I plan to do?'

His mouth twisted. 'I abhor liars, Madeleine.'

'And *I* don't like bullies, so I guess we're one for one.'

'Sit down.'

She stared at him for several seconds before swiv-elling to glance around the room. For some reason her expression tightened as she finally took in its elegance.

'No, thank you. I don't plan on being here that long.'

'You'll stay for as long as I wish you to.'

'Or for as long as it takes me to call the authorities. I came here of my own volition. I have a right to leave when I wish.'

'We seem to be going around in circles.'

'Then I suggest you cut to the chase.'

Such fire. He would have been impressed if it hadn't been for the desperation he sensed in her.

'Very well. I want you to strike a new bargain with me.'

She froze, her eyes widening. 'Excuse me?'

'Jules is gone. Whatever deal you had with him now belongs to me.'

Her eyes narrowed. 'What is this? Some sick game of Pass the Parcel? You don't even know what the deal was.'

'Whatever it is, you didn't get it. If you had, you wouldn't have been distressed when I told you he'd left.'

Her chin lifted, tugging up the sling. Fire. Vulner-ability. Remi didn't want to be touched by either but he was explicably drawn to both.

'You're assuming a lot, aren't you?' she said.

'Am I?'

She remained silent but her defiance abated.

'Shall I call your bluff and show you the door?' he pressed.

Uncertainty flickered in her eyes before her long lashes swept down, hiding her expression yet again. 'You really came here to bring Jules back?'

'That was the main purpose of my trip, yes.'

'Then why aren't you following him? Earlier you said you'd be gone in twenty-four hours.'

'No, I said I'd be available to you for twenty-four hours. That was how long I was prepared to wait to hear your side of the story. When I made plans to come here I anticipated meeting some resistance from my brother. I gave myself ample time to get the job done.'

'You managed to dispatch him in twelve hours. So you want me to do what? Fill up your free time like a court jester?' she demanded, with an hauteur that would have impressed his etiquette instructors.

'Was that the role you agreed to play for Jules?'

Her lips pursed and her gaze fixed warily on him. 'I... I'm—'

'Spend the evening with me.'

He froze. Those weren't the words he'd intended to say, but now they were out there he didn't take them back.

She was shaking her head. 'I can't. I'm...busy,' she said, her free hand rising to cradle her arm.

He dragged his gaze from that little helpless gesture, fought that bolt of protectiveness. 'Cancel your plans.' He hardened his voice. 'Didn't you have a similar arrangement with Jules?'

'No. I didn't meet him till ten—sometimes eleven.'

He despised the fact that his curiosity swelled even larger. 'That's too late. I wish to see you earlier. And you should come prepared to grant me certain assurances.'

She frowned. 'What kind of assurances?'

'The kind that require you to sign a confidentiality agreement.'

'And if I don't?'

'Then be prepared to have your life turned upside down until I'm satisfied you mean my family no harm.'

She inhaled sharply. 'Harm? Why would I…? I never meant them any harm in the first place!' she exclaimed hotly.

The affront in her tone would have reassured Remi had he not been taught a cruel lesson never to take anyone at face value. For decades he'd trusted every word that fell from his father's lips, had blindly followed where he led, right up until his true character had been revealed.

And even after that cruel betrayal he'd trusted Jules when he'd given his word that he would help protect the family legacy in danger of being ripped apart following the revelation of his father's infidelity.

Bruised and devastated from one betrayal, he'd been too grief-blind to mitigate against the possibility that he was being played again.

Jules had shown his true colours within days of being accepted into the Montegovan royal family. And then the final blow had come when he'd least expected it. All those assurances that Celeste was safe…that the worst wouldn't happen. False promises and betrayal. They had pitted his life, eroding trust until it wasn't a commodity available to him any more.

This woman, with a body that would tempt even the staunchest saint, wasn't going to sway him from what needed to be done.

'How much did Jules promise you?' he asked, in a voice spiked with ice.

The moment she inhaled sharply, he knew he'd

guessed accurately. *Money*. His insides twisted with distaste. 'Tell me how much and I'll triple it.'

Her wariness increased. 'Why?'

'I'm privy to Jules's financial status. I assure you my resources are considerably more substantial. Moreover, I can't risk you changing your mind at a later date, no matter how noble you're purporting to be right now. What better way to mitigate that than by making you a serious offer?'

She gasped. 'God, you're not just rude, you're also offensive.'

'I'm doing what it takes to ensure my family isn't held to ransom by anyone.'

The past must have bled through into his voice because her gaze sharpened. 'That happens often, does it?'

'Your insolence isn't getting us very far, Madeleine.'

A telling little expression flitted over her face at his use of her name. One that flamed the lingering heat in his body. For several moments all he could think about was whether those lips would taste as sublime as they looked, how the plump curves would feel between his teeth.

With an inward curse, he reined himself in. 'I don't have all day.'

She cleared her throat. 'I agreed to be his girlfriend in return for—'

'*Be* his girlfriend or *play* his girlfriend?' he interrupted sharply.

She swallowed. 'Play his girlfriend.'

He exhaled as a knot unravelled in his gut. 'In return for?'

'For…seventy-five thousand pounds.'

The words were hushed but the look in her eyes dared

him to denigrate her. He shoved his hands into his pockets and fought for control, but the attempt to curb his emotions wasn't as easy as he'd anticipated.

'You look as if you're ready to chew rocks, Your Eminence, but before you spit out any more insults, please know that I don't really care what you think of me.'

'It's *Your Highness*, or *Crown Prince*. Or whatever I give you permission to use at some point in the future,' he replied tightly.

'Well, whatever you call yourself, spare me that condescending look.'

'It's not condescension you see on my face, Miss Myers. It's puzzlement as to why you would sell yourself so cheaply.' The offensively paltry sum wasn't the main reason for his disgruntlement, but Remi didn't want to examine why.

She went a shade paler, and then her alluring eyes sparkled with rekindled anger. 'Excuse me?'

He allowed his gaze to drift down her body, taking in her elegant neck, her trim, tiny waist, the feminine flare of her hips and the long, shapely legs currently encased in cheap stockings.

'With the right amount of polish you could be exquisite. And I don't mean dressed in those distasteful clothes you were wearing last night. Unless you suffer from a debilitating case of low self-esteem, I believe you know this. So why sell yourself so cheaply?'

'First of all, I resent the assumption that I *sold* myself. I didn't. I agreed to play a role in return for payment. I may not be professionally trained, but I believe that's what actors and actresses do all the time. Secondly, you suggesting that I use my looks to land a better deal is frankly distasteful. I *know* what I'm worth,

Your Highness, and it has nothing to do with the configuration of my genes. Now, if you're done insulting me, I'm going to leave this place and forget you exist.'

He strolled towards her, drawn to her inner fire despite himself. 'Great speech, but I'm afraid it's not going to be as easy as that.'

'Watch me,' she returned, right before she tightened her grip on her handbag and headed for the door.

Wrapping his arm around her waist as she walked past him felt natural. Almost *too* natural. He'd only meant to detain her, but once her body was plastered to his, once he felt her warm, vibrant skin through the cotton of her shirt, his intentions altered. Not even the bolt of guilt that slammed into him made him drop his arms.

'A quarter of a million pounds,' he rasped.

Her mouth dropped open. 'W-what?' she stuttered.

'You heard me.'

She shifted in his hold, one hand rising to rest on his chest. 'You…you can't. That's too much.'

He tensed. 'Too much for what?'

Her gaze dropped from his. 'Nothing.'

He nudged her head up with a finger under her chin. 'There has to be a basis of truthfulness between us before this goes forward.'

The hand on his chest bunched, then pushed him away. Reluctantly, he released her.

'You assume something *is* going to happen between us,' she said.

'Drop the pretence. You're still as destitute now as you were this morning.'

She glided a nervous tongue-tip over her lower lip, dragging his attention again to that enticing part of her body that was chiselling away at his composure.

Perhaps his mother was right and it was time to look beyond his life of strict official duty and responsibility to the crown.

His gut tightened. From as long as he could remember, there'd been no one else for him but Celeste. He'd been satisfied with the projection of a life with her based on affection, mutual respect and dedication to his kingdom.

There'd been no over-exuberant displays of affection, but the sex had been satisfying—if a little underwhelming with the passage of time. But that had been acceptable in light of his father's extramarital affair and the claim that he'd had no control over himself.

Remi had sneered at that weakness.

He welcomed a life devoid of such emotional entanglements, and *if* his body was done with the self-imposed celibacy he'd placed upon it since Celeste's death, *if* the time had come when he could move beyond the heavy fog of guilt to the semblance of a future, he would decide with his head and not with the sharp, fevered passion that saw some men make fools of themselves. Not with the stark, blazing hunger that currently clawed at him, courtesy of the siren in front of him.

His mother had called him this morning, demanding to know who he'd selected from her list. The unspoken suggestion that there must be some sort of deadline on the guilt and grief that shrouded him had triggered a bolt of fury. His terse response had strained their conversation. But he'd hung up knowing he needed to make a decision, and soon.

But not before he'd dealt with the powder keg Jules had left behind.

'A quarter of a million pounds is much more than

the seventy-five thousand you bargained for. That and a signed confidentiality agreement means you'll get to walk away with more money than you dreamed of,' he said.

'You make me sound like a cold-hearted gold-digger,' she muttered, her words wrapped in a thin layer of something close to anguish.

But he'd seen her last night. Like in those pictures palace security had dug up, she'd been dressed for maximum effect, the wisps of nothing she wore designed to captivate any red-blooded male within her radius.

He didn't like to admit it, but the thrumming of his blood insisted he wasn't altogether immune to Madeleine Myers.

'Time is up. Yes or no?'

CHAPTER FOUR

A QUARTER OF a million pounds.

Enough for the operation her father desperately needed with plenty left over for a better place for him to live after his procedure. Surely the prospect of a brighter future would end the cycle of depression her father couldn't seem to break? It might even stretch to hiring a carer for him so she could return to university to finish her studies.

The possibilities of what that money might do staggered her for a minute, momentarily lightening the heavy weight of despair. She took a deep, relieved breath for the first time in what felt like for ever.

And then she looked into the formidable eyes watching her with thinly veiled distaste.

Relief turned to shame. A powerful need to toss his offer in his face ploughed through her. It would be immensely satisfying to walk away, prove that she wasn't the cheap little gold-digger he'd branded her. She wasn't her mother, she wanted to tell him. She didn't value her relationships based exclusively on the size of a man's bank account.

Surely he would look at her with less damning eyes if he knew the money was for her father?

A stark reminder whisked away that foolish notion.

How could she have forgotten about Greg? Friendly, cheeky Greg, who at fourteen had been one of her closest friends, part of the gang at their country club. Greg, whose wealthy parents had bred horses and looked down their noses at anyone whose personal portfolio didn't include three homes in exotic locations...

She'd been too blinded by desperation to see his true colours when she'd turned to him for support when her world had turned grey. He'd hidden his distaste well. Had fooled her with his false sympathy when she'd told him about her father. In the bleak, uncertain landscape of her new reality Greg had been her only shelter, and she'd unashamedly leaned on him in the months after her mother's desertion when the unvarnished truth of her father's addiction had come to light.

For months Maddie had trusted him with everything.

Right up until he'd hit her with the callous truth.

Greg's betrayal had decimated not just her heart but her trust. Her only consolation was that she'd never given him her body. That would have been the final humiliation.

She looked at Remi Montegova and was grateful her tongue hadn't run away with her. Men like him judged a person's worth by their prestige and status. Right from the start he'd shown his disdain at her destitution, believed she would stoop to the lowest level to achieve her avaricious ends. Even now, just like Greg, he was staring down his nose at her, demanding to know what her price was.

If she agreed to Remi's proposal she would do so with her secrets intact.

If?

In her dire position she had very little choice. She

was pretty sure the window for returning to her job at the café had closed.

She licked her dry lips, felt something hot and dark and forbidding zinging through her stomach when he followed the action. 'If I agree to this, what exactly would it entail?'

His eyes glinted momentarily, but it faded before she could decipher its meaning.

'For starters, you won't leave my sight until the confidentiality agreement is signed. After that you'll stay here in the hotel with me. I've accepted an invitation to a charity gala tonight. You'll accompany me. On Sunday you'll return with me to Montegova and stay there until I'm sure you won't change your mind and capitalise on your circumstances.'

Her stomach dropped in shock. 'What? I'm not... I can't just pick up sticks and leave!'

Silver-grey eyes narrowed. 'Why not?' he demanded. 'Perhaps because you have other commitments you're not divulging?'

The sensation in her belly intensified. 'And what if I do?'

An eerie stillness settled over him, his body becoming statue-still. Eyes the colour of threatening thunderclouds locked on her as a muscle ticked in his jaw.

'I'm not Jules, Miss Myers. I won't deal with you while you have a lover hovering in the background, ready to throw a spanner in the works.'

He walked stiff and imposing towards the door, his broad shoulders unyielding.

'Wait!'

He stilled, but didn't turn around.

'I don't have a lover. But I do have responsibilities.'

He swivelled in a smooth, regal move, those incisive eyes piercing into hers once more. 'Explain—and be quick about it.'

My God, he really was insufferable. But then weren't most people with power and authority? As much as she loved him, hadn't her father displayed a fraction of Remi's arrogance once upon a time, when he'd believed himself infallible?

'It's my father. I live with my father. I can't just… leave him.'

A fraction of that chill dissipated from his eyes, and then they grew contemplative.

'You work long hours. You're away from him for a considerable part of the day—which means that he's either able-bodied and can look after himself or he has someone else to take care of him.'

His deductions set out in clipped tones, he waited, his gaze probing hers as if daring her to refute them.

'He's able-bodied,' she said, cringing at the half-lie. 'But that doesn't mean I want to leave home for however long you intend this to be.'

He strolled with measured steps, like a predator stalking his prey, back to where she stood, frozen. 'How did your father take your liaison with Jules?'

He'd barely noticed her absence. And that was the problem. He barely noticed anything any more.

Pained wrenched at her heart. She breathed through it. 'I'm a grown woman.'

As if she'd issued an invitation his gaze swept over her body, firing charged volts everywhere it touched. By the time he returned his gaze to hers she was acutely aware of every pounding heartbeat, every unsteady breath she took.

'This thing happens only on *my* terms, Madeleine,' he stated ruthlessly.

She knew the truth behind that statement. She wasn't from his circle so he didn't trust her. What better way to keep her in check than to keep her close? Exercise his perceived right to treat her with contempt the way Greg had treated her when he'd learned the full circumstances of her fall from privilege?

But she couldn't leave her father to his own devices for long stretches. That would most certainly see him relapse before she could get him the help he needed. Unfortunately, that outcome depended on acceding to this man's wishes.

Still…

'I… I can't just pack my bags and go to Montegova with you,' she said a little desperately.

His shrug said her dilemma wasn't his concern. 'Take the next few hours to consider my offer. My driver and one of my bodyguards will take you home. You'll be brought back here at seven and you'll give me your answer then.'

Maddie took a deep breath that went nowhere near dispersing the apprehension rolling through her.

From the bodyguards and the limo to the ultra-VIP entrance to the suite she suspected was reserved for royalty, to the luxurious decadence of these rooms, everything about Remi Montegova screamed privilege and undiluted entitlement. Maddie knew that even if she walked out of here this second, she wouldn't be free of him unless he wished it.

He had determined that she was a threat to his family. One that could be neutralised by opening his wallet and keeping her prisoner for however long he pleased.

As shameful as that ultimate slur was, when it came right down to it his offer was staggeringly life-changing. All she had to do was negotiate shrewdly.

She ignored the little voice in her head that told her this performance wouldn't be straightforward—not when she couldn't look into those eyes without wild heat invading her belly. Not when she didn't even need to close her eyes to recall how it had felt to be pressed up against his hard, hot body.

But, unlike Jules's mercurial behaviour, she knew where she stood with the Crown Prince. His disdain for her was evident in every word he spoke.

Why not use that disdain as a barrier? Insulate herself in it until she got what she wanted?

With another deep breath, she forced herself to meet his gaze, even though it felt as if he was trying to strip off a layer of her skin, burrow underneath and root all her secrets.

'Okay.'

'No, Miss Myers. I want to hear the words.'

'Yes, I'll come back tonight and give you my answer.'

He stared down at her for a taut spell, an indecipherable gleam in his eyes. Then he veered away, striding over to an antique desk to pick up the phone. He relayed instructions in that curious mix of languages before replacing the handset. Minutes later, a knock came on the door.

A rake-thin man whose uniform announced his butler status appeared out of nowhere, gave a stiff bow and opened the door. The same bodyguard who'd escorted her from the nightclub last night entered the room.

'This is Antonio. He'll make sure you get where you need to go.'

In other words he'd be her shadow for the foreseeable future. It was pointless to protest.

She walked to where she'd dropped her bag earlier
and picked it up. When she turned, Remi stood behind
her. Antonio and the butler stood at a discreet distance.

'Um…is there something else?'

Remi's gaze flicked to her hair and then slowly
dragged down her body again. Dear God, the man could
strip the thoughts from her head with just the look in
his eyes.

'I'll have my stylist deliver appropriate clothes to
you.'

She nearly choked on her tongue. 'Excuse me?'

'You expect to attend a charity gala dressed as a
waitress?'

Maddie looked down at her uniform, at her threadbare tights, the worn flats.

'Of course not. But I have a perfectly adequate wardrobe.' It was a white lie. She had one classic black gown.
The rest of the designer labels her mother had pushed
upon her over the years had been sold off long ago to
pay the bills.

His face grew taut. 'If you intend to wear the clothes
my brother furnished you with, think again.'

'I don't,' she retorted, wondering at the relationship
between Remi and Jules.

She met his gaze and something within the intense
depths told her it would be wise not to ask. She shivered as he continued to look at her with an intense, almost possessive gaze.

Maddie lowered her eyes, certain she was imagining
things. Jules hadn't owned her. Remi most definitely
didn't want to. He couldn't have made that clearer with

his attitude. Nevertheless, there was something unsettling in his eyes. Something that made her breasts tingle and her belly flip-flop.

A phone rang in the background, dragging them out of the thickening sensual bubble.

Remi took a single step back. 'Good. I expect you back here at seven. Don't be late,' he said, then walked away.

Maddie didn't take a full breath until she'd shut the door of her flat behind her half an hour later. Free of Remi's disturbing vortex, the enormity of what she was contemplating overwhelmed her.

On shaky legs she entered the living room, found it empty, and approached her father's room. The door was ajar. She nudged it wider and was half relieved, half disappointed to find him asleep.

Had he been awake, what would she have said? That she'd negotiated a deal with one brother to act as his girlfriend and was now on the brink of negotiating with another for a higher sum because he believed she was a shameless, blackmailing gold-digger?

Silently, she retreated to her room, knowing that come seven tonight she would have no choice but to accept Remi's proposition or risk losing her father.

Maddie curled her fingers around the leather bound document and tried to ignore the two other people in the room. An impossible feat, of course. Everything about what she was doing evoked industrial strength butterflies in her stomach that were impossible to dismiss.

To his credit the butler, tutored in diplomacy to within an inch of his life, remained unobtrusive. Not so much his employer, the Crown Prince of Montegova, who prowled lazily in front of her as she attempted to read the fine print of the agreement.

She wanted to snap at him to be still. To be less distracting. To be less drop-dead gorgeous. Less...*everything*. But she bit her tongue. She'd agreed to this and there was no going back. Nor was there any point in denying that Remi's effect on her was shockingly visceral enough to stop her breath every time he crossed her vision.

It would wear off. It had to. No one could carry off that level of saturated charisma and power indefinitely!

She'd ignore him, just as she had all the unwanted attention that had come her way in the café. She snorted under her breath, wondering what Remi would think of being compared to the greasy construction workers and overly familiar salesman who patronised her workplace.

Her *ex*-workplace.

The inescapable reminder that she was now jobless and temporarily relocated to Remi's hotel rammed home. Her fingers shook as she recalled her conversation with her father. He'd barely responded to her carefully constructed explanation of why she would be away for two days, his absent nods when she told him that Mrs Jennings would be staying over to keep him company the only indication that he'd heard her.

For an unguarded moment Maddie wished she had a close friend to confide in. Then she wouldn't feel so dammed alone. But all her so-called friends had deserted her the moment the Myers family had fallen on hard times.

Greg had taken it a step further and kicked her in the most brutal way when she was down. His betrayal had eroded her trust to nothing and ensured she had nothing in reserve to offer anyone else when he'd coaxed her into emptying her bank account and shrugged off the risky investment that had lost her everything under the banner of 'it happens'.

Her bitter thoughts scattered when Remi approached, impatience stamped on his face. He'd given her fifteen minutes to read the confidentiality agreement, with the offer of an independent lawyer should she need it. That time had passed five minutes ago.

If she played her cards right her father could be on his way to surgery in a matter of days.

'Are you ready to sign?' Remi asked.

Her eyes jerked to his face, as seemed to happen automatically whenever he spoke. It was as if his whole body was a powerful magnet, drawing her to him. And once she was drawn, it was impossible to look away.

God, was it normal for one man to be graced with such good looks? Sculpted cheekbones, ruggedly cut jaw and glossy hair notwithstanding, it was that aura of raw masculinity that triggered the wild fluttering in her belly. She watched, enthralled against her will, as one eyebrow slowly lifted, his expression growing mocking at her unashamed perusal.

Face flaming, she dropped her gaze and grimaced inwardly when she saw he was holding out a pen to her.

The moment of truth. 'Um…'

'Percy has other duties to attend to. If you'd be so kind as to express yourself better I can ask him to stay or leave.'

She snatched the pen from him, flipped the document to the last page and signed it. Within a minute it had been signed by Remi and witnessed by Percy the butler.

When the door shut behind Percy her gaze swung to the man who effectively, according to their agreement, owned her for the next six weeks.

He was watching her too, but after a moment his gaze dropped to travel over her body, taking in her new attire.

An hour after she returned home she'd answered her door to be handed a large package by Antonio.

She couldn't help but glance down at herself. The bodice and straps of the peach-coloured gown were layered in a bandage design that clung to her shoulders, torso and hips in an intimate caress before the silky material fell to her ankles.

She didn't want to recall the heat she'd glimpsed in Remi's eyes when he'd first seen her, but the memory burned now as she withstood his scrutiny.

She wasn't going to get attached to any of this glitz and glamour. Once this was behind her there would be no place in her life for social events that involved wearing five-thousand-pound dresses and shoes.

'Did you receive my email?' he demanded.

Along with the dress, he'd sent her a new phone—one with only one number programmed into it. *His.*

She'd barely had it for ten minutes before his email had arrived. It had contained details of the charity gala, including who would be in attendance, the reason behind the fundraiser and the menu that would be served. It wasn't clear whether this was royal protocol or Remi was a control freak. Most likely a bit of both.

'Yes, I did. All read and understood, Your Highness.' She couldn't quite help the hint of sarcasm in her tone.

His eyes gleamed. 'When we're alone you may call me Remi.'

'And you may call me Maddie.'

He inclined his head in a regal nod, then prowled towards her, his face set in uncompromising lines. 'All I ask, Madeleine, is that you apply a little bit of that polish you have exhibited on the outside to the inside too.'

The barb pricked, wedging itself firmly under her skin. 'You don't want the evening to start off with insults, do you?' she asked.

'I want the evening to start off by us not turning up late,' he rasped, before heading for the door. He threw it open and glanced pointedly at her.

Maddie followed, the body-skimming dress and the effects of walking in four-inch heels causing her hips to sway self-consciously.

She watched his gaze drop momentarily down her body before he looked away.

They left the suite and rode down in the lift in a charged silence she wasn't in the mood to disperse. She was heading for the private entrance when his hand snaked around her waist.

'Where are you going?' Remi asked.

The heat of his hand against her silk-covered skin rendered her speechless for a moment. 'I thought... Aren't you using your private access?'

'What's the point? I was seen with you last night—and this afternoon at your former workplace. Believe me, every angle has already been covered by the media. Evasion tactics are no longer necessary.'

She bit her lip. 'And you're okay with that?'

'Ultimately it's no one's business *what* you are to me, but if you're asked go with the truth. We met through Jules.'

She grimaced. 'And let them all think that I'm a slapper who's jumped from one brother to the other?'

'I find stating the truth, no matter how brutal, is better than ambivalence.'

Maddie wasn't given time to process his words. The moment they stepped through the revolving doors his fingers tightened around her waist, sending her sizzling senses into full-blown fireworks.

Her breath caught at the pulse-racing effect of such a simple gesture. But then nothing about this man was simple. Everything screamed complicated and mind-boggling excitement. The only thing lacking was the *Keep Off* signs that should have been stamped all over his impeccable tuxedo.

The sensation was only heightened when they slid into the dark interior of the limo, and even after quickly positioning herself as far away from him as possible she was immediately engulfed in his deep, intoxicating scent.

What on earth was wrong with her?

'How is your arm?' Remi asked.

She stared at him, stupefied, for a moment before his words sank in. The doctor had advised that as long as she didn't aggravate her arm she could go without the sling for short periods.

'It's fine.'

The intensity in his eyes didn't abate. 'Did you take your medication?'

His brusque concern threatened to wrap itself around the protected core inside her. But, like the intricate web of lies Greg had wrapped around her for his own twisted amusement, she knew the Crown Prince's guise was false too.

'Can we dispense with the pretence?'

Silver eyes hardened. 'Pretence?'

She nodded. 'You pretending to care about me. I'm

a conniving little gold-digger, remember? And, while we're at it, I don't think you touching me in public is strictly necessary, so let's cut that false courtesy too.'

For the longest stretch he remained silent. 'I will touch you when I deem it necessary in public. And you will not object because you have signed an agreement that ties you to me for the next six weeks,' he stated, in a deep, imperious voice that drilled mercilessly into her senses.

The unshakeable knowledge that he could draw such a visceral, unfettered response from her any time he chose was shockingly unsettling.

Even more unnerving was the fact that a large part of her wasn't recoiling from that thrilling possibility.

'Then you won't mind if I reciprocate?' she dared, striving to ignore the anticipation firing her blood. 'A gold-digger needs to earn her money, after all.'

'It's a shame I'll never have the pleasure of seeing this insolence tamed out of you one day,' he mused dryly.

The reminder that he would be out of her life in a few short weeks silenced her. And when his phone rang, she listened as Remi conducted a conversation in a tense but lyrical mix of French and Italian.

Montegovan.

She stared at his proud, unforgiving profile, reflecting the genes passed down by his warrior ancestors.

Whatever was being discussed wasn't to his liking. His rugged jaw clenched multiple times before he squeezed the bridge of his nose. Then the phone call ended abruptly.

Miles went by in silence. Silence that gave her too much time to make dangerous observations, like how his strong, elegant fingers rested on his taut thighs, or the shape of his Adam's apple as he swallowed. The decadent sensation she'd experienced when his fingers brushed her back.

She shifted in her seat as low heat intensified in her belly. 'Everything okay?' she asked.

He glanced her way and she almost wished she hadn't spoken. Those far too incisive eyes locked on hers in the semi-darkness. 'The challenges of family rearing their head again.'

She nodded. 'Your father?'

He blinked in surprise before his eyes turned a shade cooler. 'My father died ten years ago.'

Her heart lurched. 'Oh… I'm sorry for your loss.'

He acknowledged her sympathy with a regal tilt of his head.

Unwilling to let the dangerous silence return, she cleared her throat. 'So who was that?'

'That was my mother—the Queen. Doing what she does best,' he said, with the faintest trace of bitterness.

'Which is?'

'Issuing edicts and expecting me to fall in line,' he mused darkly.

Maddie hid a grimace. From their very first encounter she'd known that no one dictated to this man. Whatever was being asked of him, he would counter it with merciless determination.

'What of your own mother?' he asked.

She started in surprise. 'What?'

He shifted sideways and her mouth dried as the stunning perfection of the Crown Prince was fully focused on her. 'Your mother,' he repeated.

A vice tightened around her chest. 'She's no longer

in the picture,' she replied, hoping he would drop the subject.

But he was an all-powerful prince, used to getting his way.

'Why not?'

She contemplated resisting—except he'd answered her question just now. 'We weren't always…destitute. My father used to own a thriving property business. Then the bottom fell out of the market. His business went under and we went from living in a ten-bedroom mansion in Surrey to a tiny flat in inner-city London.' Her shrug didn't quite hit the mark as painful reminders hit home hard. 'My mother didn't take the change of circumstances well. She left my father when I was in university.'

'She didn't just leave your father. She left you too,' he stated.

Her breath caught at the unexpected gruff gentleness in his voice. She'd expected a detached response, a callous dismissal of her pain, but his gaze didn't hold any censure.

'That's not all, is it?' he murmured, those eyes that saw too much boring into her.

She snatched in a breath, the urge to unburden herself swelling inside her. 'Does it matter?' she asked, attempting to reel herself in.

His answer was forestalled by their arrival. But not before he shot her a fierce glance.

Exiting the car, he turned to help her out.

The disquieting sensation increased as she stepped out to an explosion of flashbulbs. Rapid-fire questions flew at her.

'Who are you?'

'What are you to the Crown Prince?'
'How long have you two been together?'

She noticed the questions aimed at Remi were more subdued and a whole lot more respectful. Not that he answered any of them. He looked through the throng as if it didn't exist, and with a suave shift of his body shielded her injured arm and wrapped his hand around her waist again.

Nudged against the hard column of his body, she felt hers screech into awareness as they travelled along the red carpet.

After a few steps he glanced down at her for a long moment. There was a look in his eyes that tightened the muscles in her belly.

'Are you okay?'

She jerked out a nod, reminding herself sternly that it was all an act.

Still, it didn't calm the butterflies as she entered the impressive lobby of the five-star hotel hosting the gala.

According to his email, the fundraiser was in aid of establishing sports facilities for disabled children in half a dozen developing countries. When Remi introduced her to the chairwoman of the foundation, Maddie threw herself into finding out everything she could about the work of the charity, just so she could ignore the fact that she was the avid cynosure of incredulous gazes and whispers.

She raised her chin and tried to smile through it, striving for every ounce of poise hammered into her at the nosebleedingly expensive private school her parents had enrolled her in when she was eleven.

As the evening progressed, she noticed Remi's speculative gaze straying increasingly towards her.

'Our meal hasn't been served yet, so I know I don't have spinach stuck on my teeth, or something similarly unseemly, so why are you are looking at me like that?'

He paused for a beat. 'I'm not a man who's easily surprised,' he murmured, his tone low and deep as conversation hummed around them.

That earlier sting returned. 'You think you have me precisely pegged, but you don't. My current circumstances may be deplorable to you, but perhaps you should make an effort to look beyond that. You might be surprised.'

His grey eyes grew more contemplative. 'Very well. Tell me why you dropped out of a top-level university after one term to anchor yourself to that tawdry little café.'

The unexpected question threw her enough to draw an unguarded gasp. 'It wasn't tawdry. It was…okay.'

'You almost sound as if you miss it.'

She shrugged. 'It wasn't so bad.' The hours had been a long slog, but they'd made her forget the bleakness of her existence. The free meals had helped too.

He leaned closer, bringing his heady scent deeper into her orbit. 'Tell me you're not harbouring notions of returning there at some point in the future?' he rasped with a definite bite.

'What do *you* care?'

'That place was beneath you,' he breathed.

'Careful, Your Highness, or you'll get a nosebleed up there in your high and mighty castle.'

'You're far too exquisite to be working in a place like that.'

A flare of pink rushed into her cheeks. 'You can't

say things like that,' she said, aware that a few heads were turning their way.

Without warning he reached out, brushed a finger down her heated cheek. 'Why not? It's true.'

She knew the wisest choice would be to pull away, but every cell in her body wanted to lean closer into his touch, prolong that wicked thrill flowing through her bloodstream. 'Still, no one goes around talking like that.'

'Then I'm terribly lucky not to be no one,' he said.

'God, do you hear yourself? You sound—'

'Arrogant? Conceited? If it conveys my message that I prefer your silky skin to be perfumed with expensive scents rather than recycled cooking oil, then so be it.'

The melting sensation in her belly was saved from spreading to encompass her whole body by a discreet tap on a microphone.

With almost enervating relief she jerked back into her seat, her fingers clenched tight in her lap. After a moment Remi relaxed too, directing his attention to the podium.

Ignoring the chaotic emotions churning inside her, she redirected her thoughts to what he'd said earlier about her dropping out of university.

Just how much of her past had Remi dug into? She bit the inside of her lip. If he carried on it would only be a matter of time before he uncovered the truth about her father.

She waited until the speech was over and the guests had resumed their conversation before she turned to him. 'I thought you were going to stop digging into my past now that I've agreed to your little circus?' she whispered.

His eyes pierced hers, holding her captive. 'That information was in my preliminary report. Why *did* you drop out?' he asked again.

'Why are you interested?'

His gaze swept down to her lips and lingered. 'I think perhaps we should extend the parameters of our agreement.'

Heavy, charged heat bloomed in her belly. She grew intensely aware that she wasn't sitting very far back in her seat, that only a sparse inch of space separated them. The velvety firmness of his lips was tantalisingly close. One slight move and she could brush her mouth against his.

'Extend them…how?' she managed, aware that her voice had grown embarrassingly husky.

'The bare bones of your history will do.'

Disappointment lanced through her, almost making her gasp. When she had it under reasonable control, she answered. 'You already have that—whereas I know next to nothing about you. For instance, why is everyone here surprised that you brought a date with you?'

She was close enough to see the chill in his eyes before he abruptly drew back from her. 'Probably because I haven't been seen in public with a woman in two years,' he rasped.

Mild shock fizzed through her. Remi Montegova wasn't a man who'd lack for female attention. She would bet her last tenner on it. 'May I ask why?'

The look he slanted her was filled with scepticism. 'You expect me to believe you don't *know*?'

Her breath caught at his frosted tone. 'Know what?'

'It's been almost twenty-four hours since we first

met. Most people would've satisfied their curiosity about me by now.'

Maddie wasn't about to admit her disturbingly rabid interest in him. 'I don't own a laptop, Your Highness, nor do I bother with social media any more. Also, I've been busy dealing with other things today. So, no, I haven't had time to research you.'

He stared at her for half a minute before presenting her with his impressive profile. He wasn't going to answer. Clearly the extended parameters didn't include that particular question.

But after a moment he glanced back at her. 'You're a novelty to them because the last woman I dated was my fiancée,' he stated baldly.

Her lips parted, further shock unravelling through her. Questions stormed her mind. Why had the most eligible bachelor in Europe, perhaps even the world, not dated for two years? And who and where *was* the woman once promised to him?

Before she could ask, he added, 'And, no, that subject isn't up for discussion. It's purely for information purposes only.'

His statement didn't stop a dozen questions from storming her brain.

She cleared her throat, strove for a safer subject that didn't threaten to consume her whole. 'If you still want to know, I was studying child psychology at university.'

Surprise flared in his eyes.

Her laughter was tinged with bitterness. 'Is it really so shocking that I'd be interested in helping children?'

'You're putting words in my mouth.'

'Deny that you had preconceived notions about me,' she dared.

His outward demeanour didn't change, but she sensed his complete withdrawal even before he turned to strike up a conversation with another guest.

Her conviction that Remi Montegova's opinion of her wasn't about to change any time soon settled deeper, and jarred more than she wanted to accept, but she managed to wrestle herself under control and smile through the next hour.

By the time after-dinner drinks commenced and a four-piece band took their place near the dance floor she was in desperate need of reprieve. About to escape to the ladies' room, she froze as Remi turned to her. He sent the man she'd been conversing with a smile full of diplomacy that didn't make it any less stiff or dismissive.

'Your first dance is mine,' he stated.

The thought of her body close to his, moving in sync with his, sent a bolt of deep awareness through her. Dangerous, arousing awareness.

She should refuse. But she found herself rising, sliding her hand into his.

Fingers firmly gripping hers, he led her to the polished dance floor to the sound of a slow waltz. Her pulse raced faster and she fought to breathe as he gently raised her injured arm and laid it against his chest. Then one hand glided around her waist, resting there as his gaze speared hers.

She followed his lead, and strove not to react to his magnetic proximity as he started to move.

Of course the Crown Prince of Montegova danced with elegant, breathtaking sophistication.

Very much aware that even more gazes were fixed on them, she attempted to find another subject for hers.

And ended up meeting those enigmatic silver-grey eyes again. Eyes that saw far too much.

'Why not just tell them you're not interested?' she asked, a little too unsettled to guard her tongue.

'Excuse me?'

'There seems to be some sort of competition going on about who can get your attention. If you're not interested, why not just let them know?'

As if on cue, a stunning redhead twirled by a few minutes later. Completely ignoring the man accompanying her, she sent Remi a sultry smile.

Spikes of irritation, and another emotion she staunchly rejected as being jealousy, impaled Maddie. 'It must be hard, having women throw themselves so blatantly at you.'

For some reason her tart observation amused him, and his sensual lips curved with the barest twitch.

'Something funny?'

'It seems I've offended you again. You didn't strike me as having delicate sensibilities before.'

'I don't,' she denied hotly, then attempted to pull herself from his arms.

'What do you think you're doing?'

'The waltz is over. Let me go, please.'

In contrast to her demand, his hand tightened on her waist. 'We're under scrutiny, Maddie. This isn't the time to make a scene.'

'Oh, really? I…'

Her words trailed off as his head dropped in a slow but inexorable descent that announced his intention to do precisely as he pleased.

She had time to move away…time to place a hand on that broad chest and stop him from doing something that she knew in her bones would intensify the cyclone tearing through her. She didn't do either.

Her breath strangled to nothing, she watched Remi Montegova's imperious head lower until his lips were a scant centimetre from hers. Her gaze locked on his and she waited, felt his breath wash over her face as he stretched out the moment until her every sense screamed with a rabid, alien hunger, before slanting his mouth over hers.

As kisses went, the hard but brief imprint of his mouth over hers shouldn't have made such a stomach-churning impact. It shouldn't have rooted her to the spot, made the music echoing in the ballroom or the people within its walls seem to disappear.

But the ferociously intense look in his eyes and the searing brand of his kiss made Maddie experience every nanosecond of it with a vividness that promised she wouldn't forget or dismiss it any time soon, and the eye contact he maintained as he delivered the searing kiss electrified her to her very toes.

As slowly as he'd commenced the thrilling assault he retreated, giving her time to absorb the shivers rolling through her, the flames flickering insistently in her belly and the wild tingling between her legs.

It was that last damning sensation that pulled her up short, helped her fill her lungs with much needed oxygen as she attempted to make sense of what had happened.

'What…what are you doing?' she whispered under her breath.

The overwhelmingly male figure before her smiled, and a hand she didn't recall releasing hers joined the other at her waist in a firm hold. 'Extending the parameters of our association,' he said.

'I don't recall agreeing to…this.'

He stepped back, his face tightening a touch. To everyone else the Crown Prince would be a picture of elegant royalty and sophistication. But she was catching glimpses of the man underneath. Beneath the façade there was ferocious determination. An iron will. And a dark anguish.

It was too overwhelming.

Before she could recover her thoughts, he settled his hand on the small of her back and led her out of the ballroom, not stopping until they were outside.

CHAPTER FIVE

OUTSIDE, A LIGHT DRIZZLE was falling, creating puddles on the pavement.

Maddie gathered the hem of her evening gown, preparing for a quick dash to the limo. But she froze as Remi stayed her with his hand, and watched, a little stunned, as he shrugged out of his tuxedo and draped it over her shoulders.

The enfolding warmth and intimacy of his body heat heightened the already surreal atmosphere, so when he stared down at her for a moment before laying a hand in the small of her back and nudging her gently towards the waiting limo, she didn't protest.

The driver hurried towards them with a large umbrella. Remi took it from him, holding it over her head as the drizzle intensified.

She attempted to tell herself the chivalrous act was for show, but the idea wouldn't stick. Unlike his half-brother, Remi exuded magnetic charm, as well as other larger-than-life characteristics, some of which set her teeth on edge. But every single one commanded attention, focused on the simple fact that he was head and shoulders above others. A man who did exactly as he pleased.

Which circled her racing thoughts back to the fiancée he'd mentioned. She was still attempting to throttle that curiosity when the limo pulled away.

The shift of air shrouded her in his scent once again. More than a little agitated, she sat up and started to shrug off his tuxedo. 'Take this back.'

He shook his head. 'No, keep it on. Your temperamental English weather is out in full force,' he quipped, nodding out of the window to where rain lashed the windows.

For a moment she watched the hypnotic diagrams the rainwater drew on the glass. For as long as she could remember she'd loved storms. She loved watching the rain wash the world clean. Now, ensconced in the limo with Remi, watching the rain fall felt almost too intimate.

She cleared her throat and turned to find him watching her. 'Can we talk about what happened? And, more importantly, can we agree that it'll never happen again?' she stressed, relieved when her voice emerged briskly.

His eyes gleamed in the dark. 'You find what I did so objectionable?'

There was a peculiar throb in his voice that sent tingles down her spine.

'I prefer to have a say in when advances like that are made on me,' she said.

'Did you have such an agreement with Jules?'

The question was fired at her.

'Excuse me?'

'You may not have responded when he kissed you, but you didn't protest either.' His intense gaze dropped to her lips. 'Did you agree that he could kiss you?'

'No! For your information, that kiss took me by surprise too. And frankly I'm done being manhandled by you and your kin. So shall we add that to the ground rules?'

'No.' His expression hardened before his gaze reconnected with hers. 'That will not be necessary because it won't happen again.'

Something irritatingly resembling disappointment pounded through her. From the moment she'd set eyes on him he'd messed with her equilibrium. The harder she tried to regain her footing, the faster she spun out of control. It needed to stop.

They pulled up to the hotel, under the thankfully wide awning erected at the front entrance. Remi didn't seem in a hurry to reclaim his jacket, and his hand returned to the small of her back the moment they stepped out of the vehicle.

Despite the stark admonition to herself to regain her equilibrium as soon as possible, she couldn't stop herself from inhaling his scent with every breath, nor halt the awareness flaring over her skin when they entered the lift.

In the mirror's reflection his shoulders looked broader beneath his pristine white shirt, the cut of his torso delineating a physique most men only dreamed about. She was so busy ogling his body she didn't notice the lift had arrived at his floor and the doors had slid open until she caught his hooded scrutiny through the mirror.

Heat flew into her cheeks, her mortification intensifying when his gaze turned chilly. But with twisted gratitude she absorbed the sharp rejection, let it throw off the haze that threatened to shroud her.

Stepping out of the lift, she shrugged off his jacket

and held it out to him. 'I don't need this any more. Thank you.' Her voice was husky with hurt but she didn't care.

He took it, the brush of his fingers stimulating another shiver that set her teeth on edge. She needed to get her faculties back under control, because this was insane.

'Goodnight, Your Highness,' she threw over her shoulder as she marched towards her suite, conscious that he was watching her. Against her will, she hesitated with one hand on the door.

'Sleep well,' was all he said before he sauntered off, one finger hooked into his jacket and a supreme confidence in his swagger that made her want to keep staring at him.

In direct contravention of that need Maddie whirled away, entered the junior suite she'd been assigned by Percy, under Remi's instruction, and shut the door behind her.

The suite was a smaller version of Remi's but no less breathtaking. Her breath caught all over again as she looked around, scrutinised the paintings and objets d'art dotted around the room. Everywhere she looked she saw a reflection of royalty, power, prestige. There was even a photo of a monarch bearing a striking resemblance to Remi shaking hands with a president.

But not even the magnificence of her surroundings could curb the tiny tremors that continued to radiate through her body as she relived their kiss. Even now her fingers itched to trace her mouth, soothe the tingles that should have passed.

An hour later, Maddie tossed and turned for the umpteenth time, punched her pillow in a vain effort to settle, then with a start realised she hadn't thought of her father all evening. She'd been so absorbed by Remi she'd forgotten to make her check-in call.

Guilt flaying her, she eyed the clock. It was after midnight. If by some miracle he'd combatted his insomnia, all she'd be doing was disturbing his rest.

She sank into the pillow, praying for similar oblivion to take her thoughts from the man who'd captivated her senses.

Her prayer wasn't answered. The moment she closed her eyes, her mind veered back to Remi. To the dance. To that kiss.

The kiss she didn't want to happen again, she reiterated to herself.

She lived with the harsh consequences of trusting her emotions every day. Greg had used their childhood friendship to betray her. And, while her agreement with Remi was signed in indelible ink, both men were of the same ilk, judging and treating those less fortunate than themselves as unworthy.

She wasn't about to make the same mistake twice.

Against her better judgment, she reached for her phone and typed his name into an internet search engine. And there, in vivid Technicolor, lay the evidence she wasn't sure was wise to see.

Celeste Bastille had been stunning, in a gentle, doe-eyed way that showed she'd been born to be the perfect foil for a man like Remi. The daughter of French and Montegovan aristocracy, she exuded poise and charm in every picture Maddie uncovered, her utter devotion to the man at her side clear in every look.

Maddie only managed to look at a few before she tossed her phone away. Remi still loved her, if that expression of guilt and anguish on his face early this evening was any indication.

Her heart lurched at the thought of what such loss would have done to a man living in the public eye. And not just any man. A crown prince with a duty to his kingdom and future throne. A crown prince who'd lost his princess.

No. Despite the fiery insanity of that kiss, she couldn't fool herself into thinking it was anything but a throwaway reaction for Remi. And henceforth her best course of action would be to have minimal, only strictly necessary contact with Remi, and keep her father at the forefront of her mind.

But as sleep took her she knew that task might be easier said than achieved.

Kissing her had been a mistake.

Remi grimaced as he swallowed a mouthful of cognac. The smooth heat did nothing to burn away the guilt riding him. Nor did it lessen the pounding arousal flooding his manhood.

To make matters worse, his desperate scramble to recall Celeste's voice, her laugh, her gentle manner, had failed him for a few shameful seconds. Replaced with vibrant green eyes, a husky laugh, a defiant chin and bee-stung lips.

He shouldn't have kissed her.

Telling himself he had done it for the cogent reason of freeing himself from unwanted attention so he could preserve Celeste's memory felt hollow in the aftermath of the savage hunger it had awakened in him.

He'd *enjoyed* the sensation of holding another woman in his arms. Tasting her warm, willing flesh. Hearing that hitch in her breathing that signalled an arousal that matched his.

Worst of all was his inability to wrestle that beast of arousal under control. But what he'd done might have worked. No doubt there would now be a scramble to find out who the woman was who'd made Crown Prince Remi Montegova act so out of character.

Because even with Celeste he'd resisted even simple public displays of affection, never mind giving in to the ravaging lust that clawed through him.

His skin tightened with guilt as the silent promise he'd made to his dying fiancée returned to haunt him. His fingers tightened around his glass. He hadn't sinned yet. Hadn't taken another woman into his heart.

But you're thinking about taking another woman to your bed.

A necessity. For the sake of his kingdom.

Excuses.

The cold blanket of grief and guilt settled more heavily as his gaze skated over the view of night-time London. The simple truth was that he'd let Celeste down. She was dead because he'd failed her.

Remi veered away from his censorious reflection in the living room window.

His mother's second phone call this afternoon, questioning his motives, had riled him. He was already aware that his inability to fully control himself around Maddie Myers might reap unpalatable consequences. His mother pointing it out hadn't pleased him. Only his assurance that he was returning home in another day had appeased her.

As for her insistence that he choose a wife…

If he rid himself of his hunger with Maddie, then on

his return home he could focus on the more rewarding task of governing Montegova.

Celeste had understood what sacrifice meant. Would she have understood this decision?

He headed for his bedroom, his every step dogged by duelling emotions of guilt and arousal. But through it all the thrill heating his blood only grew hotter.

It was still present the next morning as he flicked through the financial section of the morning paper. Sunrise had brought more coverage of him in the social pages and another call from his mother.

It had taken exactly one minute of examining the front page and its breathtaking picture of Maddie to stoke the fire in his groin and deepen the decision that had taken hold of him somewhere between dawn and sunrise.

She was a beautiful woman. There was no denying that. In his world, women like her were a dime a dozen. But there was something more about her that snagged his attention. Something that compelled his gaze now, as she approached the dining table. Something unsettling that wouldn't let him ignore the hypnotic sway of her hips and the proud rise of her breasts.

It was deeper than common lust and, whatever it was, it armed itself in preparation to battle his unrelenting guilt.

'Good morning,' she murmured when she reached him.

Remi folded the newspaper, took time to wrestle himself under control—because duty and loyalty demanded precedence over blind, red-hot lust—then took his time to assess her. She wore a blush-pink off-the-shoulder sweater that bared one creamy shoulder and

a grey knee-length skirt that cradled her hips before
flaring at the knees. Tasteful clothes, which somehow
managed to look sinfully decadent on her body.

He shifted in his seat in a vain attempt to decrease
the pressure behind his fly. 'You slept well, I hope?'
he asked.

She sat down and smiled her thanks at the coffee-
pouring Percy before deigning to glance his way. 'No,
not really.'

He frowned at the bolt of concern that shot through
him, wrestled it down until his butler had departed. 'Is
it your arm? Do you need further medical attention?'

Her sling was back in place, but she shook her head.
'No. My insomnia had less to do with my injuries and
more to do with missing my own bed.'

'Considering where you live, I find that hard to believe.'

Bright green eyes flicked to him. 'And here I was
hoping the insults wouldn't start until I'd at least armed
myself with caffeine.'

Remi's insides tightened. For some absurd reason,
this woman burrowed beneath his skin with very little
effort. It was aggravating. And peculiarly stimulating.
'Does my honesty offend you?'

'There's honesty and there's *brutal* honesty. I'm a
firm believer in using the latter as a last resort,' she
said, meeting his gaze with eyes filled with censure.

Remi felt a spark of surprise. Very few people dared
to challenge him any more. Evidently this brave creature
wanted to be one of the few. He didn't know whether to
smile or put her in her place.

'Tell me why you didn't sleep well,' he found himself demanding as he buttered a piece of toast, placed

it within reach of her left hand and did the same with a small platter of fruit.

'Thank you,' she murmured, her eyes dropping to her coffee cup. 'I promised to check in with my father last night and I forgot.'

'As you said yourself, you're a grown woman—not a teenager with a curfew.'

'Nevertheless, I made a promise and I didn't keep it.'

She was omitting an important fact. And, just like yesterday, his need to know grew to unacceptable proportions. 'You've yet to pack for Montegova. The driver will take you home this morning. Will that not suffice?'

Her gaze avoided his. 'Um…about that…' she murmured, a pinch of guilt on her face.

Foreboding and lust burned as she licked her lower lip. 'Whatever it is, spit it out,' he prompted.

'Is it…possible to have an advance on my payment?'

The stirring in his groin abated. 'Less than twenty-four hours into our agreement and you're already demanding payment?'

'I know it's not strictly what we agreed, but—'

'You demand trust and yet hold back from telling me the whole truth about your circumstances.'

A spark of anger lit her green eyes. 'Are you saying the only way you'll agree is if I let you dig where you please into my life? You think that's fair?'

He shrugged, hardening himself against the angry hurt in her eyes. 'You're naïve if you ever thought we were on an equal footing.'

Her mouth compressed, and a rough exhalation flared her delicate nostrils. 'Is that a no to my request?'

He suppressed the need to question her further, to know everything about this woman. Why couldn't he stop thinking about her? Why, even now, did he want to lean across the table and fuse his mouth to hers?

'How much do you need?'

Again her tongue flicked over her bottom lip. 'Ten percent.'

Twenty-five thousand pounds. Not much in the grand scheme of things, but it could buy her a clean exit from his life. The urge to say no clambered through him. But a look into those stormy eyes told him she would stand her ground, fight for what she wanted.

Admiration flared through him again, but he throttled it back. He wasn't here to laud the few admirable qualities Maddie possessed. What he wanted was further leverage for his own purpose—because he had no intention of letting her get away.

'Very well. You will get what you need. In return, I have a condition of my own.'

Her eyes widened. 'What?'

He shook his head. 'We'll discuss it tonight. I have an appointment to get to.'

She worried at her lower lip with her teeth. It took a great deal of control for him not to stare.

'What if I don't like your condition?' she asked, with the tiniest quiver in her voice that Remi wanted to hear over and over again.

He stood before that battering temptation overwhelmed him. 'It's an offer of a lifetime. I'm confident you will agree. But if I'm wrong…' He shrugged. 'Then we'll revert to our previous agreement. The funds will be in your account within the hour.'

'I… Thank you.'

Against his will, his gaze moved over her face, her throat, the increased rise and fall of her breasts. The thought of tasting those lips again fired bolts of lightning through his bloodstream.

His blatant scrutiny made her colour heighten. He curled his fist against the need to trace her pink flesh.

'I trust you won't take my money and disappear?'

The challenging spark returned to her eyes as her chin lifted defiantly. 'I'm not going to keep proving myself to you. You can choose to trust me. Or not.'

Remi was still mulling over their conversation three hours later, as he sat down to lunch with his ambassador to the United Kingdom.

Maddie's fearless, plucky attitude would land her in hot water one day. Or make her irresistible to a man who was drawn to her fiery spirit. A man who would be free to kiss those intoxicating lips, mould her breathtaking curves…

He sucked in a breath, shifted as his manhood stirred to life.

Dio, what the hell was wrong with him?

He'd liked his life with Celeste. Had enjoyed her genteel nature, her generous acceptance of the challenges of being associated with a crown prince.

Nevertheless, hadn't he wished that on occasion that she would challenge him more? Stand up for what she really wanted? Offer stimulating conversation instead of smilingly acceding to his wishes?

He stiffened, disgusted with himself for dishonouring her memory. His fiancée had been loved by everyone she'd come into contact with. He wouldn't sully her memory by comparing her to Maddie—a woman full of secrets. Full of fire. Full of hidden depths he wanted to explore.

With mounting frustration he snapped his napkin open, startling the ambassador. But, no matter how much he threw himself into their nitty-gritty discussion of geo-politics, he couldn't get the woman with the defiant green eyes and Cupid's bow lips out of his head.

Which was probably why he was still disgruntled when he returned to his hotel suite. His mood plummeted further when he found Maddie nowhere in sight.

He turned as Percy entered the room and subtly cleared his throat. 'Where is she?' he all but snapped.

'Miss Myers hasn't returned since she left this morning, Your Highness.'

Stomach-hollowing disappointment replaced his disgruntlement. 'She didn't return for lunch?' he asked sharply.

'No, Your Highness.'

She'd dared him to trust her. And he had. So much for thinking she was even a fraction of the woman Celeste had been.

Dismissing Percy, he plucked his phone from his pocket and dialled her number. Her husky voice directed him to leave a message.

Remi's mood blackened. He'd been well and truly duped. Considering she'd gone from being almost penniless to being twenty-five thousand pounds richer, courtesy of the wire transfer he'd approved, she could be anywhere by now.

The reason why she'd absconded with such a paltry sum when she could have been infinitely richer didn't even puzzle him. He'd seen her bank account, knew she'd been destitute. Desperately so. And he'd handed her the tools to leave him.

His jaw gritted. She wouldn't get away with it. They had an agreement.

About to summon his security chief, he froze at the sound of approaching footsteps.

She arrived on a whirlwind of silk and heels, her face flushed, a few wisps of hair escaping its sleek knot. Even flustered and flushed, she was a captivating sight. He stared, a fever sweeping through his veins.

'Where the hell have you been?' he snarled.

She screeched to a halt, her breathlessness drawing his gaze to her chest. 'Sorry, I—'

'And why did your phone go to voicemail?'

Her wide gaze dropped to the bag in her hand. 'Oh, no. I'm sorry. I forgot to turn it back on.'

His eyes narrowed. 'Back on? After what?' Again that spike of jealousy came from nowhere. 'Tell me where you've been, Maddie.'

She blinked, her face growing wary at his icy tone. 'I was with my father. He wasn't feeling well after…after we went to the estate agents to secure our new place.'

He frowned. 'You're moving house?'

She nodded. 'That's why I needed the money. For a down payment and to get the rental process started. Then I had to start packing. The whole thing took longer than I expected. I turned my phone off so I wouldn't be disturbed.'

'Considering I'm the only one supposed to have access to you, am I to assume you didn't want *me* to disturb you?'

'I just…needed to concentrate on my father, okay?'

'Why?'

She hesitated for a beat, then took a deep breath. 'My

father isn't well. Everything took longer than I expected. But I'm here now...'

Wary green eyes met his. He loathed the wave of relief that swept through him. It strongly indicated something weighty he didn't want to acknowledge. Something compellingly close to possessiveness.

She shifted on her feet, commanding his attention.

'So are we okay? Or does that granite-hard jaw and the tight grip on your phone mean you're about to ask for your money back? If so, I won't be able to oblige. A good chunk of it is gone,' she informed him.

She was here now. He needed to let it go. But too many emotions still churned through him.

'If I'm not about to be summarily dismissed, can I ask a favour?' she asked.

'I suggest you quit while you're ahead. Or do you enjoy testing me?'

The merest hint of a smile curved lips glistening with whatever gloss she'd employed. With an elegant pirou-ette that wouldn't have been amiss in a ballet dancer, she turned away.

'Fine. I need help with my zip, but I'll ask Percy to give me a hand, shall I?' she asked, with a look over her shoulder.

His attention dropped to her bare shoulders and the silky-smooth expanse of her back. When he dragged his gaze back to her face she was staring at him with a hint of challenge in her eyes.

Dio, she could give the most notorious siren a run for her money.

She took a step towards the kitchen Percy had made his domain.

'Madeleine.'

Uttering her name was meant to be a warning. Instead it triggered something darker, more potent in the air. She stilled, her gaze widening as she watched him. 'Yes?'

'Stay.'

He approached without sensing his feet move. Her perfume filled his ravenous senses, stabbing him with a need to lower his head to that control-wrecking curve where her neck met her shoulder.

His not quite steady fingers found the zipper, slowly glided it upward while his hungry gaze roved over her light gold skin as the garment came together.

He barely heard her husky *thank you* over the loud drumming in his ears, and the sight of her cleavage when she turned to face him threatened to flay him.

Dio, this was getting out of hand.

'So, are we good?' she asked again.

'No,' he growled. 'We're late. And getting later by the second.'

She reached up to smooth back the wisp of hair that had escaped. When she dropped her arm she was the epitome of charm, poise and lethal temptation.

'Then what are waiting for?'

'This,' he muttered.

Like a starving man, he curled his hand over her nape and tugged her close. Wrapping his arm around her waist, he slanted his mouth over hers, his tongue delving between her lips as he attempted to slake his gutting hunger.

She froze against him for a single moment before her arms crept around his neck. Remi dragged her closer, slavish need sending him up in flames. When the weight of her firm breasts settled against his chest he groaned. His shaft thickened, his blood roiling as he tasted her deeply, heard her breathless whimper against his lips.

She was exquisite. Magnificent. And he wanted her more than he'd wanted anything for a long time.

They weren't going to make the first act of the opera. Their host would be disappointed but he would understand—because Remi was the Crown Prince of Montegova, after all. He would send ahead his apologies.

In a minute.

After he'd taken the edge off this insane hunger.

Maddie was barely aware of being lifted off her feet and carried out of the living room. Her senses attempted to return when Remi set her down next to a wide divan in the private living room attached to his bedroom.

Drunk on lust, she watched him tug off his tie and toss it away. Her skin grew tight, her whole body trembling in the peculiar fever only this man evoked. She curled her fingers in the soft expensive cloth for support.

'You know how phones work, Maddie. I expect you to pick up when I call. Understood?'

She blinked. 'Yes. In the future I will. But I've already apologised. Are you going to keep bullying me about it?'

Yes, she risked infuriating him further, but she couldn't seem to stop playing with fire where he was concerned. It wasn't surprising, therefore, when he prowled towards her, every masculine inch of him streamlined with purpose.

'I've never bullied anyone in my life. Whatever I've

asked of you, you've given willingly, have you not? I don't intend that to change…especially in respect of our future liaisons,' he drawled.

She didn't want to know about those. She *really* didn't. 'Whatever you think they are, keep them to yourself. Why are we in here?' she asked breathlessly.

'Are you sure you don't know?' he taunted softly, staring down at her with single-minded purpose that made her senses jump.

His hands wrapped around her upper arms, sending sensual shockwaves rippling to her very toes.

'Remi, what are you doing?' Her voice was a panting rush.

'Seeing if I can free myself from this insanity,' he said darkly.

'What…what insanity?'

He didn't answer. Not vocally. He plastered her body against his hard length, searing her mouth in a kiss that erased her every last thought.

Every warning she'd armed herself with withered and died. With a helpless moan she wrapped her arms around his neck, jerking onto her tiptoes so she wouldn't miss a second of his kiss.

When he pushed her back onto the divan she went willingly, her senses on fire. He broke away abruptly, stared at her with eyes that glinted with a touch of bewilderment. Then he took her mouth again, kissing her with a wild, frenzied intensity as his hands roamed unapologetically over her body.

Maddie felt that same bewilderment flare through her, but it wasn't enough to stop the freight train of her desire. For now, the whys didn't matter. Especially not when he cupped her breast, moulded her yearning flesh for several teasing seconds before dragging his fingers over the tight peak.

She cried out, her own fingers digging beneath the lapels of his jacket to explore the tight muscles of his shoulders.

With an impatient growl, he levered himself off her, shrugged off the offending garment and tossed it away. Eyes glued to hers, he nudged her legs apart. Heat rushed into her face as his gaze slowly dropped to where her dress had ridden up her thighs.

One impatient hand pushed the material higher, exposing the tops of her garter belt and the lacy panties already growing damp with need.

He made a rough sound under his breath. Then he settled himself over her, the rigid column of his erection imprinting itself unashamedly against her damp centre as he fused his mouth to hers once more.

Time grew elastic. All Maddie knew was that she was at the point of screaming her need, of begging him to ease the terrible ache at her core when he reached between them and boldly cupped her sex.

He swallowed her hot gasp, his tongue flicking erotically against hers as his hand delved beneath the lace of her panties. Expert fingers grazed the swollen bundle of nerves and her whole body burned furnace-hot. She wasn't aware that her nails had dug into his shoulders until he flinched and raised his head.

For a taut moment, stormy eyes stared down at her. 'How are you doing this to me?' he muttered thickly, as another whisper of guilty bewilderment flickered over his face.

Her face flamed. 'I... I'm...'

He shook his head, denying her stuttered response.

Still staring at her, he let his fingers explore, circling her slowly, erotically. Another whimper burst from her throat and, seeing the single-minded purpose on his face, she felt a tiny sliver of apprehension pierce through her desire.

He was touching her where no other man had.

Suddenly the virginity she'd pushed to one side in her fight for survival became a precious commodity she didn't want to throw away on a quick fumble. Certainly not with a man who looked at her with guilt-laden eyes.

She grabbed his wrist, halting the wicked onslaught between her thighs. 'Remi...'

He stilled, his eyes widening a fraction as he slowly exhaled. 'You want me to stop?' he breathed in quiet astonishment, as if he couldn't believe it.

She couldn't believe it either. 'I...' The denial that had surged so true in her head moments ago faltered.

His free hand spiked into her hair and his lips found the sensitive area beneath her ear. Delirium heightened and she fought to breathe.

'I don't know why I crave you like this. If you really want me to stop, say so,' he rasped in her ear.

She squeezed her eyes shut, absorbing the thrilling shiver that coursed through her before she attempted to find her voice again. 'I'm not stopping you... I'm... I don't know...' She paused, self-consciousness pummelling her. 'I'm a virgin,' she finally blurted.

He reared back as if he'd been shot, expelling a stunned breath as he stared down at her. With hectic colour staining his cheeks, and hair dishevelled from her frenzied exploration, he was the most spectacular sight she'd ever seen.

Maddie wanted to rise up, explore more of him before this thing inevitably ended. But then that skilful hand began to move again. Slowly. Tortuously.

'Tell me why you're twenty-four and still a virgin,' he demanded, his grey eyes almost black with stormy desire.

The pleasure strumming through her almost made her vision blur. 'Before you jump to conclusions—no, I haven't been waiting around for the perfect opportunity to hand my virginity to a crown prince. You're… You don't have the monopoly on emotional challenges. I was let down by someone I trusted. After that sex became…inconsequential.'

That wave of possessiveness washed over his face again, and then, his eyes still boring into hers, his touch intensified. There was something mind-melting about having him watch every whimper of pleasure he drew from her.

By the time he circled one finger at her entrance, she was a mindless wreck. She wasn't going to pass out. She refused to. She wanted to remember every second of this ride. Because it had to stop soon.

'Whoever he was, did he make you feel like this?' he rasped gruffly.

Her hair unravelled further as she shook her head. 'Never,' she whispered.

'Do you want me to stop?'

She swallowed. 'No…'

Pure male satisfaction flared over his face. Then, before she could wrestle back the last of her sanity and put a stop to this madness, his finger slid inside her. Slowly. Carefully. Ensuring she felt every breath-stealing second of invasion.

Her muscles clenched around him, greedily absorbing the giddy sensation. Then Remi touched the barrier of her innocence and the look on his face was transformed again, eclipsing all previous emotions.

Her heart lurched, thumped wildly against her ribs as she deciphered it. Shock. Hunger. *Possessiveness*. Raw and unadulterated.

She shouldn't be feeling so exhilarated. Shouldn't be allowing that fever to rage even more fiercely through her bloodstream.

'*Dio mio, veramente exquisitivo,*' he breathed.

'Remi...'

'Be calm, my beautiful innocent. I'll safeguard your treasure,' he muttered thickly.

He didn't remove his touch. Instead he levered himself over her, that enthralling finger moving in and out of her as he started to kiss her again, his tongue mimicking the action of his finger.

Maddie had no warning, no way to prepare herself when bliss shattered what remained of her world. With her fingers buried in his hair, Maddie gave herself over to intoxicating sensation, a slave to the magic of his fingers as he sent her soaring high.

She was aware that a hoarse scream ripped from her but she didn't care. It was all she could do to hold on to him as her world exploded in fragments of colour.

When she came to, she was alone on the sofa. Remi stood framed between the two heavy drapes at the window, his gaze on the street below. Whether he was granting her time to compose herself or was once again caught in the grip of furious guilt—she suspected the latter—she was thankful for the reprieve.

Quickly she straightened her clothes, passed a shaky hand over her hair just as he turned around. For a full minute he simply looked at her, until a different, more self-conscious flame rushed over her skin.

'Why are you looking at me like that?' she asked, the shakiness racking her body infusing her voice.

'You're a beautiful and desirable woman.' His voice was heavy, gravel-rough.

Her skin burned hotter. 'That sounds like an accusation.'

His hand slashed the air. 'Perhaps I'm still trying to understand—'

'Look there's no great mystery, okay? I had a boyfriend—'

'A *boyfriend*?' He spat out the word as if it was poisonous, his eyebrows knotting in a thunderous frown.

'Yes, you know what those are, don't you?'

Her sarcasm bounced off him, his expression remaining the same as he slid his hands into his pockets. 'Tell me. I want to know.'

'Greg and I grew up together. I thought we were friends. We fell out of touch for a while, but when I needed a friend I called him. We grew...close. I thought I was in a trusting relationship with him. Until I found out my plight was fodder for his amusement with his rich friends. Not only that, turns out Greg makes a habit of seeking out women and talking them into taking risky financial ventures with his company. Unfortunately I was one of those naïve victims.'

Maddie couldn't disguise her bitterness, nor shake off the heavy weight of her own failure and Greg's betrayal. She'd trusted him enough to hand over the last of her father's savings, with his reassurance that his stockbroking firm would double her money within a few months, ensuring she would have enough for his rehabilitation, filling her with wild hope.

She'd lost everything.

Remi exhaled sharply. 'Did you report him to the authorities?'

She shrugged again. 'It was all above-board, apparently. Greg claimed I'd willingly signed on the dotted line and that I knew the high risk of the investments he was making on my behalf. There was just enough truth in his story and, using our history, he convinced the authorities that I was a bitter ex-girlfriend with a grudge. He got away with it. And I was left with nothing but the clothes on my back and, yes, my virginity.'

Remi walked towards her, his eyes fixed on her face. 'Is he the reason you're caught in this lifestyle?' he asked thinly.

'It would be easy to blame everything on him. But, no, he just happened to be one straw in the bundle that eventually broke me.'

One sleekly masculine eyebrow rose. 'You think yourself broken?'

She shrugged. 'I'm currently living with a strange man who likes to throw his weight about, berate me when I'm fifteen minutes late and is paying me for the privilege. What would you call that?'

'I call it negotiating for what you want without compromising what's important to you. And I'm not strange,' he tagged on.

Maddie bit her lip against the smile that wanted to escape. 'Careful, Remi, or I might think you respect me.'

The corner of his mouth twitched for half a second

before that bewildered frown returned ten-fold and he turned away sharply.

'There you go, treating me like I'm a leper again.'

He froze. 'What are you talking about?'

She shook her head. 'What happened on the sofa wasn't planned, so if you're going to hate yourself for it could you please do it elsewhere?'

She wasn't completely sure that she wouldn't welcome a repeat, despite the polarising vibes now emanating from Remi. And just what did that say about her willpower?

'Maddie—'

'If we're not going out, I'd like to go to my suite now, please,' she interrupted, not sure she could take any more of that look on his face.

For another long moment he stared narrow-eyed at her, until stinging awareness grew into unbearable proportions. He opened his mouth, but before he could speak his phone burst to life.

He stared at the screen with a mixture of grim resolution and irritation. 'I need to take this call. Then we'll talk. Yes?'

Licking her lips, Maddie nodded, managing to hold herself together until he left the room. Then she hightailed it to her suite on embarrassingly shaky legs.

She was staring into space, her senses roiling out of control, when her own phone rang.

It was with trembling hands and an unfocused mind that she answered. It took a minute for Mrs Jennings's distressed tones to sink in. And as Maddie rushed for the door she was almost grateful for the distraction of this new bombshell that had been thrown into her life.

Because now she didn't have to dwell on the terrifying knowledge that what she'd just experienced with Remi Montegova had fundamentally changed her. And that there might be no going back.

CHAPTER SIX

REMI SUPPRESSED ANOTHER groan as he stepped out of his dressing room and headed back into his private living room. At the ringtone announcing his mother's call, part of him had relished the news he intended to give her, even though he knew she would resist it. But he'd already warned her he would do things his way.

With the charged tension between them, he'd been reluctant to leave Maddie, and he'd almost changed his mind on seeing the lingering arousal in her eyes. Remembering the taste of her. Her unfettered responses. Her tight innocence.

The cold shower he'd taken minutes ago, after cancelling his invitation to the opera, was rendered useless as his body surged in fiery recollection. He quickened his steps. And arrived in an empty room.

Maddie wasn't in the main living room. Or in her suite.

'Where is she?' He repeated his earlier question to Percy when he rushed into the kitchen. Only this time he instinctively knew he would like the answer even less than last time.

'She's gone, Your Highness. She requested a taxi fifteen minutes ago.'

Remi attempted to rein in his irritating alarm as he dialled Maddie's phone. The request to leave a message reminded him that she'd confessed to switching her phone off. They'd been distracted by other matters before she could turn it on again.

Anger rising, he picked up the suite's phone and dialled Raoul, his chief of security.

'Where is she?' he snapped for a third time.

'She's in a taxi heading south, Your Highness.'

'Why did she leave?' Remi despised the intensity of the disquieting sensation.

'She didn't say, Your Highness. She only said to tell you something came up.'

Remi took a long, deep breath, aware of his fraying control. 'Did something happen this afternoon? Something to indicate what was suddenly so urgent?' he breathed.

'I'm sorry, Your Highness. I don't know.'

Fury cut through his disquiet. But even that was unwelcome. He was far too wrapped up in Maddie Myers. And yet he couldn't locate an off switch. That cloying need to know everything about her smash through him again.

Dio, he was being irrational. The woman had a right to her secrets, whatever they were. But the sensation wouldn't go away. The discovery of her innocence had revealed another facet of her character that stunned him. But his admiration for Maddie for standing on her own two feet in the face of her challenges was also the reason he was annoyed with her now.

And, call him a chauvinist, but her streak of independence was beginning to grate as badly as her absence. After the pleasure he'd given her, after watching her come apart so spectacularly in his arms, would it hurt her to yield to him a little?

His mouth firmed even as his shaft stiffened at the reminder of what they'd shared on his sofa. He'd felt her innocence. Felt it and experienced a primitive urge to claim it.

He wasn't ashamed to admit the discovery had taken him completely by surprise, that even the thought that he would be betraying Celeste's memory hadn't been enough to dissipate the untamed hunger that prowled through him even now.

Last night, when a cold shower hadn't frozen the hunger or dispatched the guilt that had settled on his shoulders, he'd forced himself to take another path, to think rationally about the problem he faced.

The call with his mother had settled that once and for all.

He refocused. 'I'm coming downstairs. You know where she's headed. Take me to her.'

'Immediately, Your Highness,' Raoul replied.

He slammed the phone down and cursed Maddie's elusiveness.

Even though he'd never taken advantage of it, the privilege of his birth included never having to pursue a woman. Women of standing and gold-diggers alike made no bones about their willingness to fall into his bed at the slightest display of interest.

Barely an hour ago Maddie had succumbed to his caresses—then immediately dismissed him. He was finding that a…unique experience. One he didn't wish to repeat.

Irritation intensifying, he dialled her number again. For the third time her smoky tones directed him to leave a message. He tossed the phone away, his teeth meeting in a hard clench.

She'd better not to be with another man. *Or what?* The voice in his head taunted. *He'd go against all his breeding and make a scene?*

Why not? *She was his.*

Remi froze as the enormity of those three words hooked into him, unshakeable and real.

As he tried to breathe through the dizzying sensation his phone rang again. He snatched it up. Leaden disappointment seized his gut when he saw his mother's number displayed on the screen. For the first time in his life, Remi did something un-prince-like. He ignored the Queen's summons.

His mood hadn't improved one iota by the time they turned into the street he'd delivered Maddie to after their first meeting. He exited the vehicle and followed Raoul to the shabby, nondescript entrance to a tiny ground-floor flat. The door before him was thin and insubstantial, with peeling green paint.

Swallowing his distaste, he leaned on the bell, gratified when he heard a jangle of sound within. The sight of a dishevelled Maddie immediately reversed that sensation.

'What are you doing here?' she blurted, with a hasty look over her shoulder.

'You will let me in,' he instructed.

Her chin lifted. 'Will I?'

'Unless you want your neighbours to witness our conversation, yes.'

Her gaze darted past him to the six bodyguards stationed on the street and the sleek convoy of his motorcade, which was already drawing attention.

'Or you can just get back into your vehicle and leave?' she suggested hopefully.

His gut churned harder. 'I'm not leaving. This will go easier if you let me in.'

Her face paled a little but she stood her ground. 'I'd really rather not.'

'For both our sakes, I hope you didn't leave my bed to be with another man.' The very thought of it sent a spike of anger and jealousy through Remi.

Her eyes widened with shock, then anger. 'You think I left you to come to another man?'

He didn't—not completely. But the possessive beast holding him prisoner wouldn't let go, and nor would the thought that, having touched her innocence, she belonged to *him*, no matter how irrational both notions were.

He tried clinical reason. The decision he'd made would slake this unrelenting hunger within him so things could settle back to rationality. So he could focus on his duty and obligation to his crown. Where was the harm in that?

The harm is your betrayal.

The gentle voice in his head drew ice over his roiling emotions.

Remi exhaled and reasoned with it. It wasn't a betrayal if his kingdom needed him. He'd been tasked to find a solution. It was as simple as that.

He focused on Maddie's face. 'You left without telling me, after agreeing to stay. You'll pardon me if I don't have the fullest confidence in you right now.'

'I left because I had an emergency,' she replied hotly. 'I didn't think you'd appreciate me stomping into your bathroom to inform you.'

'What about using the phone I gave you?'

She mangled her lip again, drawing his attention to the swollen curve he'd kissed less than two hours ago. His groin tightened, and he felt that hot flash of lust flooding him again.

'I wasn't exactly thinking straight, all right?'

A rustle of noise from inside the flat made her tense. Nervous, she attempted to minimise the space between herself and the door.

'You have five seconds to let me in before I walk away, Maddie. You'll recall I had another proposition to discuss with you. But if I leave both our agreement and the new proposal will go away.'

She hesitated another moment before her gaze boldly met his. 'I'll let you in—but, for the record, I won't be judged. If I see so much as a trace of judgement on your face, this is over.'

The urge to remind her who she was talking to reared up, but Remi found himself nodding, agreeing to her terms of entry.

She released the door and stepped back to reveal a dank hallway with threadbare carpets and more peeling paint on the walls. It offended his every sensibility to know she lived in this appalling place. She didn't belong here. She belonged in a palace, among the finest things in life, draped in silks and sparkling jewellery, being fed the best gourmet meals and treats that would produce her thousand-watt smile.

Most of all she belonged in a world where that anxiety on her face was taken away for ever.

He wanted to be the one to do that for her.

Remi stiffened in shock at the direction of his

thoughts, then assured himself that his reasoning dove-tailed with his own goals.

'I guess you've changed your mind,' she said, a flicker of hurt mingling with disappointment at his re-action to her surroundings.

He blocked the door before she could shut it in his face, stepped inside and shut it firmly behind him. He stared down at her, breathing in the alluring perfume that still clung to her despite being in this dismal place. Her elegant throat moved in a swallow, her fingers fidg-eting with the folds of her dress. He wanted to plaster her against that dirty wall, lose himself in her the way he'd craved to do in his suite.

Another rustle from inside reminded him they weren't alone.

Abruptly, she turned and hurried down the hall.

Remi followed, arriving in a shabby living room full of mismatched dilapidated furniture and packing boxes, to find her crouching over a shrunken figure.

'I think the water spilled on the floor,' the figure croaked.

'It's fine. I'll take care of it,' Maddie murmured softly.

Remi took in the scene. The man couldn't be more than fifty years old, although he looked much older and in an appalling state of health. Nevertheless, the familial resemblance was evident from the eyes that took him in for one unfocused moment before sliding away to Maddie.

'Who's this?' the man asked.

Remi stepped forward, extending his hand to the man wearing threadbare clothes that hung on his bony figure. 'I'm Remirez Montegova. You must be Mad-die's father.'

The older man's lips twisted, his gaze resting heavily on his daughter. 'You would think *she* was the parent, the way she chivvies me. Perhaps you can talk some sense into her—get her to give me what I need.'

'What you need is rest,' she replied firmly, although Remi caught the slight wobble in her chin.

Remi took a closer look at the man, his gut tightening at the evidence of addiction.

'I'll get you some more water,' Maddie said.

She picked up a plastic cup and hurried out of the room. Remi followed.

The kitchen was in a worse state than the living room, but again he swallowed his distaste as Maddie turned around.

'Whatever you're going to say, save it.'

'Very well, I won't ask if you have the necessary health shots to survive living in a place like this. Instead I'll ask how long you think you can keep your father on that sofa when it's clear he needs advanced medical attention?'

Anger and frustration sparked fire in her eyes. 'You think I don't *know* what he needs?' She lifted a shaky hand to her temple. 'I had a system in place. It wasn't brilliant but it was working—until…'

'Until?' he bit out.

Despair replaced her anger. 'He's been so good,' she whispered. 'We were almost there.'

'He's relapsed?' Remi guessed accurately.

She nodded miserably. 'Now the hospital won't take him.'

'What hospital?'

'The one I was taking him to for a kidney transplant.'

She shook her head and picked up the cup with a shaky hand. 'Why am I even telling you any of this?'

He stepped forward and took the cup from her before she dropped it. For one unguarded moment he basked in the added leverage he'd been granted. Then he was reminded of life's cruelties, and the wisdom of seizing opportunities when they arose. At some point between last night and this morning he'd decided this woman was the answer to his dilemma. He wasn't about to be swayed by softer feelings.

He set the cup down.

'What are you doing?' she demanded. 'I have to—'

'Your father doesn't need water. He needs urgent care.'

'Yes—the kind that requires money!'

His eyes narrowed. 'The money I'm paying you?'

'Of course. Why else would I subject myself to your presence?' she sniped.

Remi wanted to kiss those insolent lips, run his mouth, his tongue, his teeth over her flawless skin and keep going until he possessed her completely.

He suppressed the wild craving. Just as he suppressed the guilt. For whatever reason, this lust had a hold on him for now, but he knew the moment he had her the thrill would be over. For now he needed to concentrate on achieving his immediate goals.

'What I'm paying you will be nowhere near enough to give him the proper care he requires.'

She frowned. 'Of course it will. I spoke to the hospital myself. I know exactly what I need.'

'Does that include long-term after-care? Does it include a contingency plan if he rejects the organ? Or treating the myriad complications that could arise?

What about now he's relapsed? How long was he to remain clean before they would perform the operation?'

'Six months,' she whispered, her face paler than before.

'So you're going sit around for another six months before you can reschedule?'

'Enough with the questions. I really don't need you to point out my problems to me.'

'Good. Then allow me to provide a solution.'

Wary blue eyes met his. 'What?'

He pushed his hands into his pockets, took a step back from her so he could think more clearly without the enthralling scent of her warm, perfumed skin fracturing his thoughts. 'There's a clinic in Switzerland, funded by my family. It's secluded, with state-of-the-art facilities, and most importantly discretion is guaranteed.'

'Don't tell me—it's where you royals go to dry out when you fall off your gilded wagons?'

Remi remained silent. He wasn't about to confirm that Jules had been the main reason for their association with the Swiss clinic.

'Why are you taunting me with this medical wonderland?' she asked guardedly, her arms around her middle.

A deep twinge lanced his chest. He ruthlessly suppressed it. He was providing an immediate solution to a dire problem. One that suited them both.

'It isn't a taunt. I can have your father there within the next twenty-four hours.'

She sucked a breath. 'Why are you helping me? My problems have nothing to do with you, and if I recall correctly I've agreed to do what I need to do to earn my keep.'

'Because I require your services for longer.'

Her eyes narrowed. 'How much longer?'

He hesitated, simply because he hadn't considered this. How long? Long enough to appease his people? His mother? His own desire for her?

The latter would scorch itself out sooner rather than later. The hotter the passion, the quicker it burned out, right? As for his mother—she'd come round to his idea too. As she'd said, they'd both been seduced by the idea of for ever, only to be disappointed by fate. This time he intended to use his head rather than his heart.

Which only left the well-being of his people. They'd been through one scandal in the recent past. Montegova required stability. Not stability that would cost him a lifetime but for the foreseeable future nevertheless.

'Remi? What sort of services?' There was apprehension in her voice, but also hope.

The twinge dissipated and he breathed more easily. 'I'll ensure your father receives the treatment he needs to get him back on his feet. You need never worry about him again.'

She took an unsteady breath. 'And in return…?' she pressed again.

'In return, I want you to marry me.'

Maddie had misheard him. This was cruel payback for her abrupt departure from the hotel. His irritation on arrival on her doorstep, her unwillingness to allow him in, his distaste at being subjected to the evidence of her destitution… All of it amounted to this…this humourless joke at her expense.

The fact that her heart had stopped for several exhilarating seconds, that she'd wanted to snatch the words from the air, hold them in her heart, was equally cruel.

Remi wanted her. She wasn't blind to that fact. But this... What he'd said...

She shook her head. 'The door is behind you, Remi. Feel free to use it.'

Brackets formed around his mouth as he stared her down with intense displeasure. 'Excuse me? Perhaps you didn't hear—'

'I heard you just fine. And I don't appreciate you wasting my time with your jokes—'

'You think my asking you to marry me is amusing?'

Laughter erupted from her throat before she could stop it. She regretted it almost immediately. In her defence, she needed a coping mechanism against the wild hope that surged when he'd said those words.

I want you to marry me.

Cold reality set in. She looked around the tattered grey kitchen that strained to contain the powerful, endlessly magnetic royal planted in the middle of it. There were no visible contaminants, so she wasn't hallucinating. No. Remi Montegova was in complete control of his faculties. And the force of his stare strongly suggested that he was awaiting her answer.

Dear God. 'You're not joking?'

His nostrils flared, a sure sign that he was offended by her response. 'I assure you I am not.'

'But...that doesn't make sense.'

Her words triggered a shift in his expression. An understanding, almost. He nodded. 'Perhaps I went about this the wrong way. I need to explain.'

'Please do,' she encouraged, still unable to believe her ears.

His gaze flicked to the grimy window before returning to her. 'After my father's death we uncovered his extramarital affairs and the existence of Jules. It caused a lot of instability within the kingdom. My marriage and coronation were supposed to allay that but then...' His jaw tightened. 'Then I lost Celeste and I had to put off taking the throne.'

'Why does that matter? Your people still love you, surely?'

Something flickered through his eyes, but his demeanour remained austere. 'My mother wants to step down from the throne,' he announced solemnly.

The unexpected revelation drew a gasp. 'That means you'll be...king.'

He nodded. 'It's not exactly news, but it seems there's a new urgency now.'

'Why?'

'The Montegovan people are forward-thinking in many ways, but they're also traditionalists. They would prefer a widowed monarch than an unmarried one.'

'You mean they think you're unsuitable because you're single?'

He shrugged. 'To them I may be king, but I'm also just a man, subject to the weaknesses of the flesh. They don't expect me to live a monk-like existence. And, as my father proved, even married monarchs aren't infallible.'

The idea of Remi with a faceless woman shot a dart of anguish through her. She struggled to keep it from showing. 'So to take the throne you need to be married?'

'In the face of the challenges my family is currently facing, yes.'

She snatched in another shaky breath. 'And you think

choosing someone like me to be your…your *wife* is the answer?' Even saying the word left her a little dazed. 'Didn't I read somewhere that you have a handy list of potential brides to choose from?'

His features clenched. 'I won't be dictated to on who I choose as my wife and Queen.'

Her heart stuttered again. 'Are you telling me there aren't committees and meetings and strategising before royal marriages are arranged?'

He remained silent for a minute. The atmosphere throbbed with charged emotions before he spoke. 'Celeste and I met at a tea party thrown by the royal housekeeper for her grandson when I was six and she was three. My mother didn't believe in separating the staff's children from the royal children. Celeste could easily have been the granddaughter of the stable manager and we would still have been engaged to marry.'

'But she wasn't, was she? She was part of your world, approved by your mother,' she insisted.

'I didn't ask for her approval then. I am not asking for it now.'

The knot in Maddie's belly tightened as he spoke of his fiancée. She fought to see things from his point of view of cold rationality. They had mutual problems that demanded a solution. Still a cold breeze washed over her.

'It's that simple for you? That clinical?'

A grim smile twisted his lips. 'It's best if I approach this with my eyes wide open.'

As opposed to being in love? As opposed to swearing his undying devotion to the woman who was now six feet under and would probably hold his heart for ever?

The chill intensified within her and she shook her

head. 'Even if I wanted to marry you—and I don't—all you would be doing would be inviting more speculation about you…about your choice of bride.'

His face slowly hardened. 'Is that your final answer?'

She opened her mouth to say no, it *wasn't* her final answer. She needed time to wrap her head around the shocking concept. To get herself on safe ground after the bombshell of his question.

Maddie closed her mouth again. With a deep breath, she looked deep into his eyes, searched his features. And with an unshakeable force she realised he truly meant it. Remi Montegova really was asking her to marry him.

She shook her head.

For several seconds he said nothing, those vivid eyes fixed on her face. When it got too much to bear, she dragged her gaze away. In the carefree days of her childhood, she'd daydreamed like most girls about that special moment when the man of her dreams would propose to her.

Not for a single second had she imagined it would be a clinical proposition from a real-life crown prince in the middle of a decrepit kitchen in a near-derelict flat.

'Maddie.' Her name was a burst of icy impatience.

She shook her head again. 'I'm sorry—'

The words were barely out of her mouth before he turned and strode purposefully out of the kitchen. She remained frozen in place, the shock of his abrupt departure holding her prisoner until the sound of a hacking cough ripped through the air.

She came to her senses with a gasp, the stark reminder of her father's condition and the growing dread that the only solution to his recovery was walking out the door galvanising her into movement.

Somewhere between rushing out of the kitchen and throwing herself against the front door to stop Remi from opening it, she wondered if she'd been struck with some sort of madness. But what choice did she have? Her father wouldn't make it for another six months.

So she placed herself before him, forced herself to look up into the stone-hard, brutally gorgeous face of Crown Prince Remi Montegova and said one word. 'Wait.'

One very regal, very haughty eyebrow lifted. 'You need to say more. I wish to hear the words, Maddie.'

'Are…are you sure this is what you want?'

Ruthless determination blazed through his eyes. 'I'm sure of what I want. Be sure of what *you* want and tell me.'

Maddie swallowed, and with the strongest notion that she was stepping into a dangerous abyss she whispered, 'I'll marry you.'

CHAPTER SEVEN

MADDIE CLENCHED HER jaw tight against the urge to take the words back, to step away from the precipice of the wild unknown upon which she somehow found herself poised. But an even greater power kept her rooted to the spot, kept her words locked in her throat as she stared up at the man she'd just agreed to marry.

In turn, he stared down at her, the light that gleamed in his eyes moments ago gone, and in its place a flat regard that set a whole new wave of anxiety blooming beneath her skin.

What had she done?

She finally managed to unglue her tongue, but before she could speak he stepped up to her. One hand rose, hovered next to her face before his fingers slowly brushed her cheek, her neck, rested on her shoulders.

'A word of advice before this thing goes forward, Maddie. This is merely a transaction—a marriage of convenience for the sake of Montegova and my people. It would be wise not to think any more of it.'

Something withered and died inside her—something she hadn't even known existed until she'd lost it. The yawing emptiness it left behind made her furiously regroup, tighten the reins around her scattered emotions.

'Are you warning me not to fall in love with you?' She infused her voice with as much haughtiness as she could and knew she'd struck the mark when his eyes narrowed.

'That is exactly what I'm saying,' he confirmed.

She inhaled shakily and for a moment was ashamed of her treacherous body and the weakness Remi evoked within her. Was it that same weakness Greg had seen in her and taken advantage of?

The thought straightened her spine. 'Thank you, but that somewhat presumptuous warning isn't necessary. I've already learned my lesson once before. You may be a great catch in your royal circles, but you're not exactly my type.'

His expression morphed from coldly forbidding into…something else. Something that removed the flatness from his eyes and replaced it with a gleam of challenge.

Maddie ignored the skitter of alarm and attempted to shrug off the hand that lay too close to the pulse hammering at her throat. His hold lightened, turned into more of a caress as it drifted down her arm to rest at her elbow.

'And what exactly is your type?'

Less charismatic. Less overwhelming. Less…everything.

She didn't voice the words. He was gorgeously imperious, irresistibly arrogant enough.

A round of deep coughing shattered the thick silence, dragging her attention from the enticing magic of his touch. When she darted away from him Remi dropped his hand, but he didn't step out of her way.

'I have to go and see to my father,' she said.

'We have further issues to discuss.'

She swallowed, the enormity of what she'd agreed to hovering like an electric storm. 'I know.'

He nodded. 'But first I'll make arrangements for your father to be moved from here in the next few hours.'

Surprised by the dizzying speed of his actions, she nodded. 'Thank you.'

'I'm merely facilitating your smooth transition into my life, Maddie.'

A transaction. Nothing more. 'I'm still grateful,' she replied.

Something shifted in his gaze, but he looked away before she could decipher it. With a hand on the door, he paused. 'I expect you back in the suite by six o'clock. Pack whatever you need from this place. You will not be returning.'

He was gone by the time the mild panic freezing her vocal cords had receded. She looked around the soulless hallway, wondering if the last ten minutes had truly happened. Had she really just agreed to marry the future King of Montegova? A man who'd warned her not to fall in love with him?

The vice that had wrapped around her chest at the warning tightened. Breathing through it, she hurried into the living room. Her father had fallen into a light sleep, his chest rasping with every breath.

She'd been more frightened than shocked when she'd received Mrs Jennings's call. She had disposed of the painkillers she'd found after a frantic search, knowing full well it was already too late for her father's operation.

But it wasn't too late to save him. And if the answer was to marry Remi...

Even now she couldn't complete the overwhelming thought. Was this price too high to pay?

She stared down at her father and firmed her lips.

No price was too high.

But as she tucked a blanket around him and hurried to her room she knew that wasn't altogether true. There was a reason her instincts had warned her to stay away from Remi the first time she'd seen him in that nightclub. But, unlike her blind trust when she'd believed Greg, she was walking into this with her eyes wide open. Besides, Remi wasn't plying her with false promises.

That reassurance firmly in place, she fished out her suitcase.

Maddie took her most valued possessions—pictures and mementoes of her and her parents in happier times, the necklace they'd given her on her sixteenth birthday...

She was still locked in a semi-haze when a team of six medical staff arrived on her doorstep two hours later.

Their firm, efficient manner reassured Maddie that her father was in good hands. Her anxiety abated further when Henry accepted his new situation with surprising alacrity. He even emerged from his stupor to return her grip when she held on to him for one last minute before he was loaded into the private ambulance.

Tears filled her eyes when he caressed her cheek. 'Be all right, Dad. You're all I have. Please be all right,' she whispered fervently.

He gave her a sad smile. 'I'll do my best, sweetheart.'

'Promise me,' she insisted, even though she knew she shouldn't.

He closed his eyes for a long second. Then he nodded. 'I promise.'

The doctor stepped forward, shattering the moment. 'We'll prep your father at our Chelsea clinic in preparation for his flight to Geneva tomorrow.'

Maddie swiped at her eyes and swallowed the lump in her throat. 'It's happening that quickly?'

The doctor nodded. 'We've been instructed to get your father on the road to recovery as soon as possible.'

Remi. All afternoon, despite being gone, his presence had lingered in the form of the gleaming SUV on the street and the two bodyguards within it.

They followed her to the clinic now, and one stood outside her father's room—ready, as he'd informed her, to escort her back to the hotel.

With her father hooked up to IV fluids and falling asleep, Maddie knew she couldn't linger. The moment she stepped into the hall the bodyguard fell in behind her, steering her out through a discreet entrance and into the SUV.

What felt like only minutes later they were back at the hotel. Her already shortened breath evaporated as Remi, tall and commanding, materialised before her when the lift doors parted. With an elegant hand, he gestured to his suite. She told herself it was no use baulking at the silent command. She was doing this with her eyes wide open.

'I trust everything is all right with your father?' he asked.

She nodded, her gaze flicking to him as she sensed his repressed impatience. 'He was looking better even before I left.' She mentally crossed her fingers that it would continue.

'That's good. Sit down, Maddie.'

She sat. The quicker they got this discussion over with, the quicker she could retreat to her own suite, deal with the shock that hadn't quite abated.

Percy's arrival with a tray of drinks only added to the surreal sensation. She watched in silence as he uncorked a bottle of champagne, poured out two glasses and then with a respectful bow made himself scarce.

'Are we celebrating?'

Remi simply shrugged one shoulder. 'I'm aware that I may have appeared a little…clinical before.' He prowled over to her, one glass extended.

Maddie took it, unable to drag her gaze from his powerful leanness. 'So now you're trying to soften yourself towards me? Are you afraid I'm going to change my mind?'

'You've given me your word and I'm learning that you're a woman of your word.'

Before she'd fully absorbed that unexpected compliment, he continued.

'But I also wish to demonstrate that I will not be a complete ogre in our marriage.'

Marriage. The word still had the ability to churn her guts and rob her of breath. Which was probably why she simply bobbed her head.

'Shall we drink to that?'

There was a tightness in his voice she would have hazarded a guess was anxiety in any other man than the one standing before her. Whatever it was, it brought even more acute awareness when he lowered his body into the seat next to hers, suffusing her with his intoxicating scent.

She trembled as he clinked his glass against hers and

as she took a sip of exquisite champagne, very much aware that his eyes were fixed on her face. 'What else did you want to discuss?'

He sipped his drink too, then placed his glass on the coffee table. 'It's imperative that we make this marriage work for the sake of my people. There has to be a smooth transition when my mother steps down. Which is why we need to expedite this. You father will soon be on his way to Geneva. Even if you weren't committed elsewhere you wouldn't be able to visit him. He'll be in isolation for the next eight weeks. If we are to marry in five weeks then—'

'Five *weeks*?'

He tensed. 'You object to that?'

'I thought… You're the Crown Prince, soon to be King. Doesn't a royal wedding take months…*years* to plan?'

'My mother has been waiting two years for me to be married. She's motivated to make it happen sooner rather than later.'

The reminder that his last wedding had been brutally thwarted by tragedy dropped like an anvil between them. A glance at his face showed that forbidding expression, blocking everything else out.

Maddie knew he was undertaking this marriage out of duty to his people alone. He'd even gone so far as to tell her not to fall in love with him because his heart was committed for ever to someone else.

She quickly averted her gaze, snatched in a breath when she spotted how close she was to spilling champagne all over herself, but when she started to shift away from him he stopped her with a hand on her arm.

'One last thing.'

She gritted her teeth. 'Yes?'

'Although this isn't a love match, I expect you to act a certain way when we're in public.'

Maddie couldn't stop a bitter laugh from spilling out. 'So I'm expected to fawn over you in public, am I?'

'Within reason and the appropriate comportment, yes.'

God, he was unbelievable. 'What about you? Do you get a pass in the fawning department or is this a *quid pro quo* situation?'

He stiffened. 'Be assured I'll do my part,' he said.

Despite the weird somersaults in her tummy, she grimaced. 'Is all that really necessary?'

'It is. Part of your wedding preparation will be tutoring in the art of diplomacy.'

Unable to withstand his touch without giving away the sensations rampaging through her, Maddie rose. He remained seated, but his eyes stayed on her as she paced in front of the coffee table. When she opened her mouth, he stopped her with a commanding hand.

'If you're about to express reservations, you're wasting your time. Things may seem overwhelming at first, but I'm assured you'll rise to the occasion.'

'I'm glad one of us is confident.'

'You're twenty-four years old. You were little more than a child when the burden of taking care of your father fell on your shoulders. You turned your life inside out for him. I am confident our marriage will be far less challenging.'

Because he would never feel the wild, dizzying breadth of emotion for her that he'd felt for Celeste.

The churning inside her intensified as he rose and advanced towards her. When he cupped her cheeks, tilted her face up to his and angled his head towards hers, she stopped breathing.

Without speaking, he sealed his mouth over hers.

The kiss was thorough, deep and knee-buckling. Steel-like arms gripped her, plastering her body against his as he patiently, ruthlessly, explored her.

When it was over he raised his head. For several seconds they stared at one another as her pulse thundered in her ears.

'What…what was that for?' she eventually stuttered.

'Practice. For all the ways that count, Maddie, I expect this marriage to appear real.'

From that moment on the series of events that tripped into each other was exponentially overwhelming. Both in London and Montegova, the publicity ball was rolling forward, gathering furious momentum.

When they left the hotel for the airport the next morning, it was through the front doors, to find media interest triple the size of any they'd encountered hitherto.

'What's going on?' she asked.

'My press office have alerted the right people that my interest in you has become something…*more*.'

He didn't answer any of the media's frenzied questions, but his hold around her was proprietorial, the long look he sent her before they got into the limo possessive and sensual.

She was just reiterating to herself that this was all an act when they arrived at a private airport and she caught a glimpse of the jaw-dropping Montegovan royal jet.

Enough to accommodate several families comfortably, the two-deck plane was so opulent Maddie was afraid to touch any gleaming surface. Her sense of disquiet was intensified when, upon boarding, Remi swiftly disappeared with a clutch of officious-looking advisers.

When an elderly gentleman approached and introduced himself as a history professor, specialising in Montegovan history, Maddie was grateful for the chance not to dwell on the overwhelming things happening to her.

Over the next few hours she learnt that only Remi's direct ancestors or their queens had ruled Montegova.

Which brought a question screeching into her mind.

They hadn't discussed children or future heirs to the throne. But Remi's words from last night returned with a deeper, more frightening meaning.

'For all the ways that count, Maddie, I expect this marriage to appear real.'

Did that mean children? With her?

She was grappling with this disturbing new dynamic when Remi entered the cabin. His eyes narrowed on her as he casually dismissed the professor.

'What's wrong? You look as if you've seen a ghost.'

'I have a question,' she blurted, before she lost her nerve.

One imperious eyebrow lifted.

'I've just discovered that only your family have ruled Montegova.' She licked dry lips, attempted not to react when his gaze dropped to her mouth. 'That means you intend your own children to rule…'

Her words trailed off when a harsh, bleak look hardened his face. Something jagged slashed at her heart but she forced herself to keep breathing.

'I intended my children to take the throne one day, yes.'

Her next exhalation was decidedly shaky. 'But that means…'

'That means I'm required by law to consummate my marriage in order for it to be legitimately recognised. But when I take you to my bed on our wedding night it'll not be so you can bear my children.'

Why that only caused that wrenching ache in her heart to intensify, Maddie couldn't comprehend. It was clear that Remi needed time to come to terms with his new future. They were in the same boat.

But were they?

He was looking after his people's future, but in many ways he was stuck in the past with his dead fiancée.

The cold wave that washed over her was still present when they landed and were met by a sizeable delegation on the tarmac.

After a swathe of introductions and hearing names she would struggle to remember, they boarded a royal motorcade of sleek limos. Minutes later Maddie caught her first glimpse of the stunning capital city.

Just like everything Montegovan she'd encountered so far, Playagova was a stunning mixture of ancient and modern architecture, every corner pulsing with a rich history she was dying to explore.

But with each mile closer to the royal palace, Maddie's nerves grew tighter, until by the time they arrived at the stunningly magnificent building her pulse was racing and her fingers were a twisted mess in her lap.

Remi's long fingers reached for hers, triggering a whole new range of nerves. Ever since he'd mentioned their wedding night a deep, carnal ache had settled in her pelvis—one she couldn't suppress no matter how much she tried. And she was beginning to think it was useless to fight it any more.

She was wildly attracted to him. And he intended to possess her completely, if only for one night. Maddie shivered, then caught his sharp inhalation. Turning her head, she met his gaze full-on, unable to stop the wave of heat that engulfed her.

His eyes dropped to her lips and they parted automatically, responding to the hunger sparking between them. That hunger turned ashen when his jaw abruptly tightened and he removed his touch.

With the ghost of his fiancée placed solidly between them, Maddie was left with the distinct feeling that the non-turbulent future Remi had promised was less than certain—at least for her.

Unless she found a way to cage her emotions in this clinical marriage she'd agreed to, she risked exposing herself to a pain far greater than the pain she had suffered at Greg's hands.

She was reminding herself of that as she waited with Remi outside Queen Isadora's private dining room. Once again dressed impeccably in a bespoke suit, he was a jaw-dropping vision, with a presence that absorbed her to the exclusion of all else.

Butterflies took flight again as she cast a furtive glance at his remote expression. 'Any tips on how to deal with this?' she attempted with forced levity.

His expression didn't change. 'Simply be yourself.'

'You mean my *charming* self, don't you?'

His response was to conduct a slow, thorough perusal of her body, taking in the orange gown a palace stylist had presented her with less than an hour ago.

The capped sleeves and respectable neckline projected a classic elegance she desperately hoped for.

'You captivate whether you mean to or not, Maddie. You'll have no problems with my mother,' he rasped.

She wanted to hate him for leaving her tongue-tied once again. But she was still busy attempting to breathe as elegant double doors opened before them and a steward stepped forward.

'Her Majesty is ready to receive you,' the man announced.

The dining room held a table large enough for three dozen people. Seated at the head was the Queen of Montegova.

Eyes similar to Remi's tracked them until they reached her. Queen Isadora neither frowned nor smiled, but Maddie felt as if her every secret was displayed in bold scarlet letters above her head as she held the queen's gaze.

'Maman, it's good to see you.' Remi bowed and brushed kisses on her cheeks.

Queen Isadora ruthlessly assessed her son. 'Is it?'

'Let's not make this any more difficult than it needs to be,' Remi replied.

'I see we're dropping all semblance of diplomacy,' the queen responded, and then her gaze swung to Maddie as Remi pulled out a chair for her.

Maddie caught herself before she sat down, manners and what little she'd read of royal protocol kicking her into giving a curtsy. 'It's an honour to meet you, Your Majesty,' she murmured.

'She has manners. That's something, I suppose,' Queen Isadora quipped.

'Maman…' Remi's voice held a rumbling warning.

His mother turned sharply to him. 'This isn't how it is supposed to be. When I sent you to England to handle the Myers situation I pictured a lot more circumspection. Instead you've returned with this—'

'Your Majesty, I would be so very grateful if you wouldn't speak about me as if I'm not here.'

Two pairs of eyes turned to her, the male ones holding mocking amusement and the other a trace of shock.

Queen Isadora spoke first. 'You have fire. I'll give you that too.'

'What else will you give me, Your Majesty? If we're to be family, I'd like to know the best way to proceed without causing offence.'

Maddie caught the faintest twitch of her lips before the rigidness her son was so masterful at settled her features.

'Let's not be hasty. You are not quite family yet.'

'But she will be. I have made my decision,' Remi stated.

The implacable announcement made the queen exhale sharply. For several heartbeats silence reigned, her face paling slightly as she searched her son's face. Then something extraordinary happened.

Queen Isadora gave a deep sigh, her ramrod-straight spine relaxed and she nodded. 'Very well. If this is how it's going to be, I will accept it.'

Maddie hadn't been aware she was holding her breath until it rushed out. But then she discovered her ordeal was far from over.

For the next two hours, in between the presentation of mouthwatering dishes, the queen grilled her on everything from her childhood pets to her mother's desertion.

The discovery that Remi had kept nothing from his

mother should have upset her, but having everything out in the open, a clean slate, was liberating. She was tired of carrying the burden of her family's shameful secrets.

But even as that old weight dropped away she knew she carried a newer, more devastating one. One she didn't want to give voice to yet. If ever.

Her gaze flicked to Remi as he escorted her to her suite. She intended to keep up a full emotional guard around him. Those same instincts that had screeched a warning the moment they'd met clamoured even louder now, telling her to heed his warning against falling for him. And for as long as this sham marriage lasted she intended to do just that.

CHAPTER EIGHT

MADDIE LOOKED UP from the report she was reading about her father as Remi walked into the large living room attached to her suite. As had happened increasingly alarmingly over her last five weeks in Montegova, she felt something wild and unfettered lurch in her chest at the raw masculinity that charged from him, his predatory prowl towards her sparking every nerve ending to life.

Comforting thoughts of her father's progress gave way to a tense shakiness inside her as those eyes fixed on her with the unnerving intensity she'd come to expect. As she searched his face, Maddie also recognised other expressions, those she kept hoping would be absent when he looked at her.

She breathed out, unable to avoid the hard-edged detachment, the rigid wall he'd erected around himself almost from the moment they'd landed in Montegova. And with every day she spent in the palace she was made aware of how much Remi had loved and cherished Celeste.

From the suite of rooms in the east wing that no one entered to the Lipizzaner mare lovingly groomed each day but which no one ever rode, Remi hadn't just erected a shrine to Celeste—he'd surrounded himself with reminders of his lost love.

Each discovery had triggered a bewildering ache to Maddie's own heart, an ache that intensified the more she attempted to deny its power over her. That power was very much present right now, threatening her with a runaway pulse and shortness of breath as Remi stopped in front of her, towering and powerful.

She set the report down. 'I didn't think I'd be seeing you again today.'

They'd performed the last of their day's engagements at midday. The charity rowing competition had been well-attended, and the crowds gathering outside the grounds of the royal lake had duly been introduced to Remi's new betrothed.

To say that wedding fever had taken hold of the country was an understatement. It had even eclipsed the queen's announcement that she was stepping down from the throne—an outcome that had brought a rare, wry smile to Queen Isadora's lips.

For the first week Maddie had been stunned by her ready acceptance by Remi's people, and the endless stream of gifts arriving from far and wide in celebration of their engagement.

But that euphoria had waned when, with each passing day, she'd realised the man she was marrying wasn't in the least bit affected by the excitement, that the charm and attention he lavished on his future bride when they were out in public was just an act.

Behind closed doors Remi couldn't get away from her fast enough.

Deep down she couldn't fault him for that. He'd warned her against developing any untoward emotion.

The trouble was, Maddie was beginning to think that her heart and mind had differing plans.

'I came to give you this,' Remi said, producing a royal blue velvet box from his pocket.

'Another trinket?' she asked.

There'd been a steady procession of family heirlooms over the last week, presented to her as part of Montego-van tradition. One of several.

'Why are you doing this?' she blurted, unable to stop herself in the face of his rigid demeanour.

If anything, his expression grew even more remote. 'This belonged to my grandmother. She wore it on her wedding day.'

She waved him away. 'I don't mean whatever is in that box. Why are you marrying me if you're so un-happy about it?'

He stiffened. 'Do I need to rehash my reasons one more time?'

'I know you're doing it for your people, but surely a part of you must want this for yourself too?'

'You think I don't want this?'

'Yes, I do,' she replied boldly. 'I think you'd give al-most anything for the person you're marrying—*me*—to be somebody else. Tell me I'm wrong.'

He lost a shade of colour—the first time she'd seen Remi less than in full control. A second later his jaw clenched tight.

'That line of reasoning is useless and a waste of time. The past cannot be changed.'

She rose to face him, even though their equal foot-ing was an illusion. 'And yet you're letting it dictate your future. If you're truly not done with grieving over her then you should wait. I've met your people. They'll understand if you need to find someone else who...'

Her words fizzled away when he tossed the box onto the seat she'd just vacated and cupped her shoulders in a firm hold.

'We have an agreement. If this is your way of attempting to wriggle out of it, think again.'

'I'm trying...' She stopped and took a breath. 'No one will talk about her. Everyone whispers. They're scared of upsetting you by saying her name out loud.'

His eyes narrowed. 'What?'

'You heard me.'

His eyes burned into hers, warning her against pursuing a forbidden subject. 'You're prying into matters that don't concern you.'

She laughed—a bitter sound that scraped her throat. 'Don't concern me? Because this is supposed to be some sort of clinical transaction?'

'Precisely,' he snapped.

The ache in her heart grew. She rubbed at it with her clenched fist but it didn't dissipate. 'I'm not a robot without feelings. I can only keep up the charade for so long.'

'Is that a veiled threat?'

She sighed. 'No, it's not. It's a suggestion that you may be doing yourself and your people a disservice in the long run if this marriage they seem so happy about turns out not to be what they expect.'

His nostrils flared. 'You *dare* to tell me how to see to my own people's well-being?'

Maddie tried not to be distracted by the fingers still gripping her, branding her skin. 'I'm attempting to give you a new perspective. You shouldn't dismiss your mother's way of doing things out of hand. You never know—you may even find someone on her list you might grow to like eventually.'

'You think I don't *like* you?'

Her chest tightened. 'Do you really need me to answer that?'

He stared down at her for breathless seconds, and then with a harsh sound he yanked her close. Merciless lips seared hers, creating a path for lustful flames to consume her whole.

It had been five long weeks since that wild encounter in his suite back in London. With every touch and look he'd orchestrated in public, the hunger he'd incited in her had only intensified. And, try as she might to deny it, desire bore down on her tenfold now, rendering it impossible for her not to wrap her body around him, strain to get even closer.

One hand gripped his waist, the other spiked into his hair in a turbulent bid to intensify the kiss. He met her bold demand, thrusting his tongue into his mouth. For endless minutes they devoured each other, their hands almost frenzied in their wild caresses.

They were both panting when Remi eventually tore away from her. He didn't let go, or remove his gaze from her. 'I may not have conventional feelings towards you,' he rasped, 'but this unstoppable fever in my blood desires no one else but you. Do you understand *that*?'

With every cell in her body she wanted to claim those words, hold them close to that ache in her chest. But she couldn't. Because… 'That's just sex,' she said shakily.

'It's more than most people have.'

'And when that's gone…?'

His lips compressed. 'Then we'll find a way to co-exist in civility.'

'That can't be enough for you, surely?' she countered.

His hands dropped from her like leaden weights to fist at his sides. Maddie watched with sickening fascination as he reasserted absolute control of himself.

'For the sake of my kingdom, it has to be enough. For *your* sake, you'd better not renege on our agreement.'

She drew a breath, but before she could speak his gaze flicked to the report on the chair.

'Your father is making good progress, I understand?'

She nodded. 'Yes.'

'Let that be your defining goal, then.'

What about me? What about my heart? What about what I want?

The words remained stuck in her throat as he nodded at the velvet box. 'See you at the altar tomorrow, Madeleine. Wear the necklace. It will please me.'

He left the suite, taking the vibrancy and the oxygen out of the room. She subsided into her seat, her stomach hollowing out as she acknowledged just how much she'd wanted that conversation to go differently.

Had she really expected some indication that he'd one day get over his devastating loss? That the impenetrable fortress around his heart would crack open to let someone else in? Someone like her? How much warning did her foolish heart need? It was time to accept reality. To stop hoping for the impossible.

Hands clenched in her lap, she stared down at the velvet box. She wasn't sure whether she reached for it out of curiosity, to see what other priceless heirloom was being bestowed upon her, or whether it was because it was the last solid confirmation that come tomorrow she would be marrying Remi Montegova, as she'd promised.

For better or worse, and for however long it lasted, she was locked in this thing with Remi. Perhaps if at some point in the future his emotional detachment turned into physical detachment he might even let her go, spare them both the inconvenience of a loveless, sexless marriage.

Maddie ignored the further anguish that thought brought and stared down at the unopened box. She had to embrace this upcoming wedding wholeheartedly, put her best game face on and play her role.

Except that wasn't so easy the next morning as she stood before the bevy of attendants who'd arrived to prepare her for her wedding day.

For the last hour they'd gone about their duties with quiet efficiency, kind smiles and muted excitement, all carefully orchestrated to allay her jitters. Except the butterflies in her belly were in full kamikaze mode. No matter how she diced it, she was marrying the Crown Prince of Montegova—the man who in a few short weeks would be king.

Clinical undertaking or not, it was enough to steal the breath from her lungs—especially when her wedding gown was lowered over her head. She'd fallen in love with it on sight, picked it out of the vast selection three top Montegovan couturiers had presented her with five days after their engagement had been announced.

It was made of silk and lace, and the sweetheart neckline showed the barest hint of cleavage. The heavy material followed her form down to her knees in an elegant train of diamond-studded lace. Her arms were covered in the same lace pattern to her elbow, but at the back the design dipped in a deep vee, leaving her bare from nape to waist.

She'd been a little reticent about choosing the daring design, but her heavy lace veil would conceal the back of the dress, and for some reason she'd experienced a spark of delight at the thought of wearing this particular dress today.

Maddie suspected that the spark had come from the inadvertent discovery of Celeste's wedding dress on her one visit to the east wing. She knew she should have left the private suite that seemed suspended in time the moment she'd suspected what it was. But curiosity had overwhelmed her. And she'd known the second she'd spotted Celeste's demure heavy satin gown that she would choose differently for herself.

Perhaps that had been wrong, she pondered now as she slid nervous hands over her hips.

Whether Remi chose to acknowledge it or not, Maddie intended to stay true to herself in this marriage. In every way she intended to be her own woman—if only for the sake of her sanity.

With that affirmation, she attempted to smile as the head attendant presented her with the box that contained Remi's grandmother's wedding necklace. Awed gasps echoed in the chamber as the two-tiered diamond necklace was reverently placed around her throat and fastened. And with that final click, her time was up.

Maddie blinked hard at the tell-tale sheen in her eyes as she caught her reflection. She'd woken this morning to a profound loneliness that had left tears on her pillow. For far longer than she'd wanted she had wished her father or even her mother were by her side.

That feeling had only intensified during the long hours of preparation, until it was balled in a dull ache in her chest. So receiving a hand-delivered envelope, and opening it to see a note from her father, had drawn more heart-wrenching tears.

On one last whim she crossed to her bedside table, picked it up and re-read it.

My dear Maddie,
The past few years have been difficult for all of us, but especially for you. I haven't been there for you and I've let you down.
This note isn't about asking for forgiveness. It's about expressing my unwavering pride in you, my joy at your accomplishments and my awe at your strength.
My only regret today is that I'm not there to walk you down the aisle.
I wish you a long, happy and fruitful marriage, my dear.
As for forgiveness...perhaps one day I'll ask for it. When I'm strong enough and worthy to be called your father again.
For now, with all my love,
Dad

She treasured the note, held it dear in her heart. But the truth was that she was in this alone. Her only relief was the fact that Remi had been insistent on coming clean about her family's circumstances to avoid further scandal, and had sent out a press release about her father being in rehab. The expected furore had accompanied the news, but had died down very quickly soon after. Her past was no longer a secret, and she could walk down the aisle with her head high.

Accepting she would so alone, Maddie was stunned when she arrived at the entrance to the west wing, where her wedding carriage awaited, to find a tall, dark tower of a man bearing a striking resemblance to Remi waiting for her.

With suave elegance, he took her hand and brushed a kiss over her knuckles. 'My brother told me you were walking down the aisle alone. I came to offer my services,' he said, in the same deep voice as Remi. 'I'm Zak, by the way.'

It took a moment to locate her voice. 'Zak... It's lovely to meet you, but you don't have to,' she managed shakily.

He shook his head. 'My offer isn't completely altruistic. I'm told I've been remiss in not getting involved in the wedding preparations. The least I can do is get to know my future sister-in-law before she actually marries my brother. So shall we?'

He held out his arm to her, much as his older brother had several times since she'd met him, but without the charming smile Zak displayed now.

Maddie took a deep breath and blinked back tears. 'Thank you.'

Within minutes of settling next to him in the car, she felt her nerves come back full force, then intensify as the sheer volume of the crowd gathered to witness the ceremony overwhelmed her.

To her eternal gratitude, Zak kept the conversation light as they progressed slowly towards Duomo Montegova, the sixteenth-century cathedral reserved for royal ceremonies.

Maddie waved and smiled, but attempted to blank her mind to what was actually happening. Ironically, it was Zak's presence, reminding her that she would be his brother's wife before the hour was out, that made it impossible to get away from the fact that she was risking certain heartbreak by tying herself to a man who would never love her.

She knew she'd gone beyond risk the moment her senses leapt at her first sight of Remi, poised at the altar.

His grey morning suit was impeccable, its bespoke design highlighting his towering frame to perfection. The sweet flower girls before her, the pageboys carrying her train, the stunning lighting inside the cathedral and the soft gasps from the guests all faded away as Remi became the sole focus of her attention.

Even Zak's slight stiffening when they reached the place where a familiar-looking socialite sat with her daughters, and a brief glimpse of a young woman's pale face as she stared at Zak, didn't dilute the potency of her connection to Remi. It was a miracle that she managed to place one foot in front of the other and breathe in and out as she finally arrived in front of the man who would be her husband.

She barely heard Zak's murmured words as he handed her over to his brother. All she could feel above her thundering heartbeat was Remi's grip on hers, that intense determination in his eyes.

'You look breathtaking,' he murmured gruffly.

The words sounded sincere, but she couldn't help but wonder if he was wishing he'd said them to someone else. From behind her veil she searched his face—

a futile task, but one she couldn't seem to stop herself from conducting.

Was this destined to be her life? Searching for signs that Remi felt something for her other than duty and obligation?

A delicate throat-clearing from the priest refocused her. Automatically, she repeated the words she'd practised for the last week. The knowledge that they were final and binding forced a lump into her throat.

After several seconds Remi turned his lithe, powerful body towards hers, in a less than subtle command for her to speak her vows.

'I take thee, Remirez Alexander Montegova, to be my...husband...'

An exhalation from the crowd confirmed that hers wasn't the only breath being held at that moment. A furtive glance at Remi showed his eyes burning deeply into her face. She quickly averted her gaze, focused on repeating the remaining vows that bound her irrevocably to him.

When his turn came he spoke his vows in deep, solemn tones, with no hesitation as he slipped the wedding band onto her finger. The last of her breath was strangled in her lungs when he lifted the veil off her face. With one finger tilting up her chin, his head descended, his intention to follow tradition an immutable certainty.

The kiss was firm, branding, but over in the briefest of seconds. Still, it drew gasps and sighs as he slid his arms around her and brought his mouth to her cheek.

'Bravo—you played the game admirably. And it wasn't such an ordeal, was it?'

She plastered on a smile but didn't respond—because she couldn't. The heavy weight of the platinum and diamond wedding ring on her finger kept her mute. But she managed to keep her smile in place as Remi walked her back down the aisle and throughout the elaborate banquet, the first dance and their ride through the streets.

By the time she re-entered her suite, to change her attire for the trip to the Amber Palace—the honeymoon residence passed down from Remi's grandfather to him—her smile was frozen in place.

She'd barely touched her food, had taken no more than a few sips of the vintage champagne during the reception. Luckily no one had commented on her lack of appetite. They'd been too busy absorbing the news that Remi had truly married *her*, a commoner with unsavoury baggage in the form of a drug addict father and an absentee mother.

'Is everything all right, Your Highness?'

Maddie started, the sound of the title automatically conferred upon her on marriage stealing her breath.

She managed a small nod. 'I'm fine, thank you.'

Just a little bit longer, she told herself. *Then there will be the night to deal with.*

A different set of nerves assailed her. And it had nothing to do with the impending hot air balloon ride with Remi—the last event of their wedding ceremony— although that was daunting in itself.

When she'd learned of that aspect of the ceremony, she'd experienced a childlike thrill—right up until the moment it had dawned on her that the ride would culminate at the palace where she'd spend her wedding night.

Maddie couldn't suppress the tremor that shook her. Remi desired her. Enough to overlook her complete inexperience? And for how long?

Pushing the questions out of her mind only worked until she once again came face to face with Remi.

He'd changed into a navy suit, with a pristine white shirt and a velvet bow tie. With his hair combed neatly, and a pass of the razor over his jaw, he was a sight to behold as he took her hand and led her across the immaculate lawn towards the giant hot air balloon emblazoned with the House of Montegova's royal crest.

With one hand holding up the hem of her pale gold evening gown, she joined Remi in waving to their guests before they headed down the red carpet to board the basket.

Her every sense flared into awareness in the enclosed space as Remi stepped in behind her and signalled to the balloon technician. In minutes they were soaring into the sky, vintage champagne in hand.

The scene below her was breathtaking. Only one thing could have made this moment more special. If the man next to her had been truly and completely hers.

That thunderbolt of an admission froze her in place as Remi closed the gap between them. Strong arms arrived on either side of her, caging her in, and helplessly she breathed him in, unable to stop a shiver as his scent pervaded every atom of her being.

Her action drew a frowning look. 'I'm sorry…' he murmured solemnly.

Startled, she snapped her gaze to his and was imprisoned by fiercely gleaming eyes. 'For what?'

'I never asked whether you were okay with heights. We can land and go by car if you prefer?'

Maddie shook her head, drawing her gaze from his hypnotising one to the carpet of lights twinkling beneath them as the sun began to set.

'I'm not afraid of heights. And it's beautiful up here,' she replied, taking a sip of champagne.

He merely nodded, but she felt his gaze resting on her.

'How long is the flight?' she asked, trying to dissipate the charged tension eddying around them.

'Under an hour.'

'I'm surprised you're allowed this mode of transport. Your bodyguards must be beside themselves.'

The rarest of smiles twitched his lips, and she burned with the need to see the full force of it.

'They're close by.'

She turned her head and met his gaze again. 'Really?'

His smile widened a touch as he nodded his head over his right shoulder. A glance in that direction only showed her a speck on the horizon. On closer inspection, though, she noticed it was a helicopter, flying out of sound range.

'Have you *ever* known true privacy?'

He shrugged. 'It's easier to just let them do their thing. They know when not to intrude.' His gaze slowly raked her, returning with a banked heat that enflamed her. 'That will be as close as they will get in the next five days.'

'You mean the Amber Palace has its own security?'

He lifted his glass and took a long sip before answering. 'Do you really wish to know?'

The butterflies somersaulted in her belly. 'Why else would I ask?'

'Perhaps you're trying to avoid discussing what's coming?'

She took another large gulp of champagne in a wild

bid to steady her nerves, but the glass shook as she lowered it and read the look on his face. Remi wasn't attempting to hide his hunger for her.

'Is there any point in discussing it?' she asked, in a voice that emerged unsteadily.

He shook his head. 'No, only the absolute certainty that I will make you mine before the night is through.'

The deep timbre of his voice invaded her being, more intoxicating than the champagne in her hand. Another shiver rolled over her when his hand closed over hers, resting on the lip of the basket.

'It would please me to know that you're not attempting to get tipsy.'

'I'm not,' she said hurriedly.

'You barely touched your meal,' he stated.

'Are you trying to ruin my buzz?' she murmured.

His gaze raked her face and settled on her mouth. 'The only buzz I want you to experience is the sensation of having me buried deep inside you. I will accommodate no other.'

She swayed against him. An actual weak-at-the-knees sway that he halted with a firm hand on her waist. And there his hand stayed for the duration of their flight.

After she gave a helpless, unfettered moan.

After he leaned down and slowly, thoroughly, tasted her lips.

After she forgot about everything—including the technician whose back was discreetly turned to them as they continued to soar through the sky.

After it struck her hard that she was living the most exquisite moment of her life, with the last of the setting sun in front of her and the darkening of the capital city behind them.

Tears rose to her eyes as with their descent a boom of fireworks ripped through the sky, painting the darkening curtain of night with exhilarating colour.

She snatched in a stunned breath. 'God, it's wonderful!'

The hand branding her waist tightened and Remi pulled her close, until her back rested against his broad chest.

'Yes,' he said simply, before his lips brushed her temple.

They remained silent for the rest of the journey, until the burnt gold spires that lent the Amber Palace its name rose into view.

Smaller in scale than the official seat of the monarchy, it was no less breathtaking. But as the basket touched down next to an elaborate lamp-lit maze, set to the east of the palace grounds, there was only one thing on Maddie's mind.

Her gaze slowly rose to meet Remi's. There was no going back. This was her wedding night, and if it was all she'd ever get—duty to the Montegovan crown or not—she would take it. Treasure the experience. She would give her virginity to her husband without trepidation or regret.

CHAPTER NINE

REMI ATTEMPTED TO moderate his pace to match his new bride's as they strode through his favourite palace. Despite her avid scrutiny of her surroundings, the tell-tale tremble of the fingers caught in his announced her trepidation. On the one hand he could hurry and get this over with, so she'd see there was nothing to worry about. Or…he could stay away from her altogether.

No.

The latter was out of the question. This marriage needed to be consummated. And he… He needed to have her before he went insane.

But she looked a little pale, so he slowed his steps further, led her from one opulent living space to the other.

'How long has this been in your family?' she asked once they'd circled back into the least formal of the living rooms.

He let her extricate her fingers and engage him in conversation instead of doing what he yearned to do— which was to sweep her off her feet and stride up the stairs into the master bedroom suite.

'My great-grandmother built this as a surprise wedding present for my great-grandfather.'

Her eyes widened as her head snapped down from

where she'd been examining the murals on the ceiling. 'How long did it take to build and how on earth did she manage to keep it secret?'

Remi recalled the fond tale with a smile. 'Very carefully, with a lot of bribery and a few tantrums that ensured she would be left alone for when she needed to visit the site. She instructed the first stone to be laid the day after they were betrothed. They didn't marry for two years.'

'And did he like his surprise?'

'According to the historians, she left clues of secret passages and architectural delights that enticed him to stay for six months.'

Like the specialised jewels created in this part of his kingdom, the whole palace was decorated in different shades of amber, with expert lighting that gave the illusion of it being suspended in a field of dark gold.

'I'm not surprised he didn't want to leave. It's stunningly beautiful.'

He watched her touch the amber teardrop crystal on a nearby lamp and wanted those fingers on him.

Striding to her, he seized her hand again, lifted it to his lips. 'I will give you a fuller tour later,' he said, aware that his voice was deeper, rougher. 'Right now I have a more urgent need.'

When her lips parted on a soft pant he couldn't hold back any longer. He swept her into his arms, satisfaction oozing through him when her slim arms encircled his neck.

'What are you doing?' his sharp-clawed kitten demanded as he strode out and up the stairs. 'I… I can walk.'

He wrapped his arms tighter around her. 'I'm giv-

ing you the chance to tell your own story some day—
one that doesn't include tripping over the stairs because
your husband was too impatient with you.'

'Are…are you?' she asked, her voice tremulous, her
gaze wary.

He paused long enough to drink his fill of her undeniable beauty before mounting the last step. But that
pause also let in that little voice that said he needed to
do *more*. He'd held her at arm's length because ever
since her arrival he'd expected her to find a loophole,
get out of their agreement. He'd issued veiled threats,
left her to her own devices when he could have given
her a little more of his time and attention.

He'd noted her hesitation before she'd said her vows.
That most of all had unsettled him. If he wanted this
marriage to work, even on the basest level, he needed
to do…*more*. He negotiated challenging trade deals,
walked diplomatic tightropes all the time. So why did
the idea of *more* unnerve him?

He took a breath, and went with the carnal truth. 'I
want you, Maddie. More now than I did half an hour
ago or the moment we first met.'

Her breath shuddered out, her eyes growing several
shakes darker as she watched him.

'Would you like me to show you?'

Her nod was shy, a touch hesitant, but it still swept
fire through his veins, lent further urgency to his steps.

Within a minute they were in his private chamber,
the doors behind them firmly closed. Without setting
her down, he lowered his head and took her mouth with
his. Her soft moan set the blaze inside him higher, and
when her tongue brushed timidly over his mouth Remi
nearly lost his footing.

He'd barely lowered her down when he spiked his fingers into her bound hair. Then he dived deeper, unable to wait one more second for a taste of his wife.

His wife...

For the first time since tragedy had struck, the thought of anyone but Celeste as his wife didn't strike with oppressive pain.

Perhaps it was because the deed was done. Perhaps his physical craving for Maddie was dimming the guilt and pain. Whatever it was, he intended to take it—even if it was just for tonight.

He licked her soft, velvety lips, then stroked his tongue deeper into her mouth, absorbing her unfettered shudders as her arousal spiked to match his. He repeated the action a few times before gently nipping her tongue with his teeth. She whimpered.

'Do you like that, *piccola*?' he breathed against her lips.

'Mmm...yes.'

'Then you shall have more.'

Remi kissed her until she clung to him. Until they were both breathing hard. Until the pressure in his groin demanded further action.

He gently nudged her to the side of the bed. Then, dropping to his haunches, he tugged her shoes off. He glanced up, surprising a strange expression across her face.

'What?'

She bit her lip. 'You... Almost kneeling at my feet. Feels...weird.'

He brushed his thumb over her delicate anklebone. 'Weird good or bad?'

'Is it bad to say good?' she whispered.

Remi lifted her right foot and kissed her soft instep. A shiver raced up to engulf her whole body.

'Nothing that happens between us tonight in this room will be bad,' he responded.

Within his grasp her foot trembled, and her colour deepened. He slipped his hands beneath her gown, trailed his fingers up her legs without taking his eyes from her face.

'Why are you watching me like that?' she asked, again in the hushed whisper that had varnished her words since they entered his room.

'You're to be mine. I want to see what pleases you.'

Her flush deepened. 'Will I sound gauche if I say *everything*?'

His hands tightened convulsively on her knees as a sudden compulsive need to claim *everything* swept over him. But did he have a right to *everything* when he couldn't return the same? And why the sudden yearning for exactly that?

He shook the thoughts free, glided his hands higher up her silken flesh until he brushed the edge of her panties.

'I'll give you as much as you can take. Stand up and turn around, *piccola*.'

She obeyed. Still kneeling, he reached up and drew down her zip, exposing her supple back and delicate spine to his gaze. He kissed the base of her spine as he divested her of the dress and her bra. Then, hooking his fingers into her panties, he tugged the scrap of satin down her legs and tossed it away.

His mouth watered at the taste of her skin, the feel of her naked hips in his hands, the scent of her sex. Nudging her back around, he kissed his way up her belly to her luscious breasts as he parted her thighs and caressed his thumbs over her damp sex.

'Remi…' she moaned, her trembling intensifying as he licked and teased her nipples.

The clamouring grew too wild to resist and he drew back and pulled down the bedcovers. 'Lie down and open your legs for me. I want to taste your innocence one last time before I claim it.'

Her breathing truncated as she silently obeyed. With their gazes broken, Remi allowed himself another look at the magnificent landscape of her body, at the secret place between her thighs he intended to lay full and final claim to tonight.

Full and final?

This time the voice lingered even after he'd attempted to brush it away. Continued to linger as he nudged her slender legs high, kissed his way down her right knee, then the left. It lingered as he delivered the ultimate kiss, watched her back arch off the bed and her fingers scramble for purchase in the silk covers. It was still there when he tongued her clitoris and felt her body grow taut a moment before her climax ripped through her.

The satisfaction that mingled with his lust was unlike anything Remi had ever experienced before, and after caressing her through her release, when he rose to divest himself of his own clothes, the wild hunger rippling through him stunned him further.

He reached for a condom and was tugging it on when she slowly blinked her eyes open and sought his gaze.

'Remi…' she murmured.

Something shifted in his chest, and again his attempt to bat the sensation away felt woefully inadequate. Two steps brought him to her. He wrapped his arm beneath her and repositioned her on the pillows. Before she could speak he captured her mouth once again, eager to escape the worrisome sensations zinging through him.

He caressed her from nape to hip, with hands that weren't quite steady. When he grabbed her arms and hooked them behind his neck she immediately wrapped them around him, clung on tight.

That wild craving to have her there *always* pierced him. No doubt it was the newness of this, the novelty of her innocence. No doubt he would be rid of these absurd notions once he'd had her.

With that thought, which had more than a whiff of desperation attached to it, he slotted himself between her thighs and cupped her nape with one hand. Her lids slowly lifted, her alluring eyes meeting and clinging to his.

'Are you ready to be mine, Madeleine?'

A tremor shook through her, then she nodded. 'Yes.'

He positioned himself at her core. When her breath caught he lowered his head and delivered a gentle kiss. 'Relax, *ma petite*.'

She breathed out.

With a muted groan, Remi pushed himself inside her snug, exquisite heat.

The flash of pain that ripped through Maddie drew a scream. Mindlessly, she dug her nails into his shoulders. He flinched, and yet his next kiss was as gentle as the last.

'Be calm, Maddie. The worst is over.'

Wildly she shook her head, reluctant to breathe, reluctant to move. 'I…can't…'

'You can. You will. You're mine,' he breathed against her lips, and surged inside her once more.

Prepared for further pain, Maddie gasped as a different sensation arrived. And stayed with his next thrust.

On the sixth, bliss such as she'd never known flowed up her spine. She'd thought that night in London had opened her eyes to pleasure. And again just now, when he'd used his mouth, she had imagined she'd crested the very pinnacle of desire.

The phenomenon of Remi moving powerful and deep and relentless inside her robbed her of everything except hedonistic pleasure. His mouth at her lips, her throat, his hands holding her tight to him wrought magic. She'd asked for everything. *Everything* was turning her inside out with ecstasy.

'Oh... God!'

'*Oui...si...*'

She wouldn't have thought it possible, but the mixture of languages that formed Montegovan sounded sexier than ever, whispered in her ear by its crown prince. Her husband.

'Remi,' she gasped as he angled her hips and surged deeper.

'*Dio mio, cosi exquisitivo. Dea...*'

'Translate...please. I... I want to know...'

'You're exquisite...a goddess,' he breathed in her ear. 'I will teach you Montegovan, then you will understand...'

'Yes.' She wanted that too. *Everything*. And more.

Maybe it was foolish to ask. But she... Dear God, she was in love with him. She couldn't *not* be.

She opened her eyes, though she couldn't remember shutting them, to find his ferocious gaze fixed on her, ten times more intensely than he'd ever looked at her before. She couldn't have looked away if she'd wanted to. So she didn't.

She lost herself in his power and in their pleasure until the bough broke again. More spectacular. Vastly superior in sensation. Her scream this time was of pure ecstasy, and the fingers digging into his back pleaded for it never to cease.

He kept moving within her, kept up the sizzling tempo until he gave a long, guttural groan. His magnificent body grew taut, and then convulsions rippled through him.

For the longest stretch of time, the only sound in the suite was their snatched breaths and racing hearts. When they calmed, he withdrew from her body. Maddie barely managed to curb a whimper, and watched in silence as he left the bed and entered the adjoining bathroom.

Boneless, she collapsed on the bed, her every sense still struck by the awe of what had just happened. Was it like this every time? How soon could it happen again?

She was still drifting on a sea of sated bliss when Remi returned and scooped her up.

'What…where are you taking me?'

The sound of a bath running and the scent of bath oil drifted through her senses, answered her question.

'A bath will do you good,' he said, before lowering her into warm, jasmine-scented water.

Maddie couldn't stop the blush that suffused her face as the water closed around her. Expecting him to leave her to it, she started in surprise when he nudged her gently forward and slid in behind her. She would have thought what they'd done in the bedroom was intimate enough, but having him share her bath introduced a whole new level of intimacy that wrapped itself around her heart—much as she wanted him to wrap his arms around her.

When he did just that, a moment later, all the barriers she'd attempted to erect around her heart crumbled. She wanted this. Wanted *him*. For ever.

The weight of that need terrified her—so much so that she stiffened.

The arms around her tightened. 'Is something wrong? Are you sore?'

She pulled her knees up to her chest, shook her head as another blush flared into her cheeks. 'I'm fine,' she blurted.

'You're not,' he countermanded smoothly as he nudged her head against his shoulder. 'It's okay to be overwhelmed.'

Maddie wanted to laugh, but feared it might morph into a sob. She wasn't fine. Far from it. She was hopelessly in love with a man who would never belong to her. Perhaps even now she was on a countdown to when he'd walk away from her.

The heart that had soared minutes ago in her new marriage bed dipped alarmingly, grey despair filling the empty spaces. Terrified of giving herself away, Maddie kept her head tucked into his shoulder, not protesting when he picked up a washcloth and began gliding it over her skin.

For one absurd moment she wanted to ask whether he'd done the same for Celeste. Thankfully that curiosity passed unuttered, but it did nothing to dissipate the knot of tension in her belly as she withstood his ministrations.

Perhaps it was the warmth of the water, his powerful but gentle hands, or the acceptance that she had truly passed the point of no return, but Maddie slowly began to relax as other sensations pushed themselves to the forefront of her consciousness.

She became acutely aware of Remi's solid body enfolding hers, the back-and-forth motions of the washcloth over her breasts and belly, the slight hitch in his breathing. She didn't know what prompted her to lift her head, glance up into his face. Once she did, she couldn't look away.

They stared at each other for an interminable minute before his gaze raked over her face to rest on her lips. Unable to stop herself, she lifted her hand to his taut cheek, wild need urging her to explore further. She smoothed her thumb over his lips, his faintly stubbled chin, the bridge of his patrician nose, the sleek wings of his eyebrows. He was perfection, and she wanted to weep with the heartrending knowledge that he would never be hers.

But he's here now. He's yours for now.

She felt his manhood stir against her hip and gasped at the renewed thrill in her veins. Seeing the fierce hunger in his eyes, she drew her hand down his neck, over his superbly honed chest and hard six-pack. There she hesitated, her face flaming all over again at the thought of touching him so intimately.

'Touch me, *dea*,' he encouraged thickly.

Goddess. That was what he'd said the word meant.

Her insides melted. It was dangerous to be this affected by the endearment, but it was already too late. The word flowed into her heart, joined all the other pieces of gentleness and desire and attention she'd received from him.

Like a miser tucking away precious gems, Maddie gathered every scrap and stored them in her heart. She would need them one day, maybe one day far too soon, when he turned away from her.

She slid her hand over his hot skin, beneath the water to his groin, her breath dissolving in her lungs as she grasped his thick girth.

His hiss of arousal made her flinch, but the look in his eyes encouraged her to continue on her path. Emboldened, she grasped him more firmly, explored his glorious length until he hissed again.

'Enough, *dea*,' he ground out.

She wasn't ready for this sensational moment to be over just yet. 'Please…' she whispered, even though she expected him to stop her.

His answer was to spike his fingers in her hair and angle her face up before plundering her lips with his. Time ceased to matter as he kissed her with a fierce thoroughness that left them both breathing hard when he abruptly ended the kiss and repositioned her over his lap.

Maddie clung tightly to his shoulders as his steely length nudged her core. Just as before, the first probe was gentle, insistent—and breathtaking. His gaze stayed on her face, absorbing her every reaction as he slowly penetrated her once more, strong hands gripping her hips for his possession.

Maddie gasped as all the sensations from before came screaming back. And with no prospect of pain this time, the pleasure was tenfold.

Tears rose in her eyes as bliss suffused her. When he rocked her into movement, when she understood the advantage of her position, she began to move over him.

He grunted—a thick, masculine sound that filled her with feminine power. That power might be fleeting and feeble at best, but it still lent her enough impetus to take him deeper, to glide her fingers into his hair and notch his head up for the addictive kiss only he could provide.

Remi gave her what she wanted and more, one hand rising to cup her breast and torment its peak as he kissed and possessed her. Within minutes they were careening towards that unstoppable summit, scented water splashing around them as he introduced her to a whole new level of pleasure. Guttural Montegovan words fell from his lips as he edged her higher, and she opened her heart, letting his words spill into those greedy spaces.

Nirvana arrived in a thrilling rush that went on for ever. Beneath her, Remi gave a rough shout in the steamy space as he charged through his own climax.

She welcomed the strong arms that bound her and held her close, and as their heartbeats slowed she dared to hope that perhaps they had something to build on after all. Perhaps if they had this, in time they would have something more. Because surely he couldn't be this affected, this intimate with her, without considering handing over even a small piece of himself?

She would find a way to make him happy in any way she could. In the hope that one day he might truly see her, even love her.

That bleak little voice mocked her again, called her ten kinds of fool for attempting to compete with a ghost.

But surely there was a way for her to show Remi that, while she would never replace the woman he'd lost, she could be something meaningful to him eventually?

She was so absorbed with her frantic plans to make her new husband love her that she didn't realise he'd stiffened beneath her until a curse she didn't understand but knew for its harsh iciness ripped through the room.

She froze. 'Remi...?'

He rose from the water with her in his arms as if she weighed nothing. His face was turned away from her but she didn't need to look into his eyes to tell that something was terribly wrong. The clenched jaw, the tension bracketing his mouth and the thunderous, forbidding frown evidenced that something was definitely amiss.

It took all of three seconds for her to clue into what was wrong. 'Oh...God...'

'*Si,*' he hissed icily.

Stepping out of the bath, he disengaged from her and placed her back in the water. Unable to stomach the horror on his face, she hugged her knees.

They hadn't used protection. They'd been so caught up in the moment that crucial part of it had gone out of their minds. At least that was her suspicion.

A furtive glance showed his deepening horror. 'Remi...'

'No,' he breathed, spiking his fingers through his hair.

'What does *no* mean, exactly?' she asked.

He responded with a string of Montegovan words that meant nothing to her.

'Translate. Please.'

He strode across the room, snatched up a towel, wrapped it around his hips. Still with his back to her, he sucked in a tortured breath. 'How could I?'

'How could you what?' she asked tremulously.

He swivelled to face her. 'Be so damned careless.'

Her head dipped a fraction, her heart hammering at his bleak tone. 'We both were, Remi.'

His hand slashed the air. 'I don't mean *you*. I was careless with *her*. I promised myself I would never be careless again. And now I have done it again. With you.'

She flinched. 'You mean Celeste?' He was bringing his dead fiancée into *this*? She wasn't sure whether to be furious or desolate. She chose the former. 'It's our wedding night, Remi. It might not mean anything to you, but it means something to me. How can you bring her into this moment?'

'What?' His brows clamped together as if she was speaking an alien tongue.

Perhaps she was. Bitter laughter ripped from her throat. 'What was I thinking?' she murmured to herself. 'This is how our marriage is going to be, isn't it?'

His frown deepened. 'What are you talking about?'

'Don't pretend you don't know. How can you not know when she informs your every decision? How can you not know when you never stop thinking about her?'

Fierce eyes narrowed. 'Maddie—'

'No,' she interrupted, equally fiercely. With a strength she hadn't known she possessed, she rose out of the bath, her gaze fixed on his as she stepped out. 'How do you think it makes me feel when the first thing you think about when you're faced with a crisis is *her*?'

His head went back as if she'd struck him. For a moment she wished she had, if only to knock a little bit of sense into him.

'Calm down—'

'Why should I? You just dismissed me out of hand. Even though this is happening to *both* of us, you didn't even think about me.'

His expression grew even more arctic. 'If I hurt your feelings—'

'*If?* Look at me, Remi. Do you actually see me standing here in front of you?' she asked, in a voice that reflected the anguish tearing through her.

A muscle ticked in his jaw. 'Of course I do. Don't be absurd.'

'I'm being *absurd*, am I? Perhaps next you're going to call me melodramatic for having feelings? For wanting a say in my own marriage?'

'Protecting you is my prerogative,' he replied tersely. 'My priority.'

Just like it was with Celeste. He didn't need to say the words.

She battled to keep the anguish from ripping her asunder. 'Can we talk about this like two rational human beings? *Please?*' she tacked on at the absolutely implacable look on his face.

He stared at her for a charged moment and then nodded brusquely.

About to speak, Maddie realised she was still stark naked. He realised it too, his gaze heatedly raking her body before, veering away sharply, he snagged a robe and held it out to her.

She started to reach for it.

The wave of dizziness came out of nowhere, snatching the strength from her knees and the air from her lungs.

With a shocked, guttural curse, Remi lunged for her, locking her into his arms as her body crumpled.

'*Dio mio,*' he cursed thickly. 'Are you okay?'

The dizziness dissipated as quickly as it had arrived, leaving her senses clear. 'Let me go. I'm fine.'

'No, you are not.' Robe discarded, he swept her up and strode back into the bedroom, placing her on the bed before stepping back. 'We will talk after you've had something to eat and rested.'

'No, I want to talk *now*.'

He seared her with a blistering, imperious gaze that reminded her that in everything but the coronation ceremony he was the King.

'Some things you have a say in, Maddie. The subject of your health and well-being, especially when you're neglecting them, isn't one of them. You barely ate anything all day long, and indulged in new experiences on top of that. If you wish for a rational discussion then you'll do as you're told.'

She tugged the sheets up to cover herself even as she raised her chin in defiance. 'Are you calling me irrational?'

His face closed up even more and he expelled a harsh breath. 'I'm recommending we talk when emotions are less heightened.'

With that he strode into his dressing room. He emerged five minutes later, dressed in the most casual attire she'd seen him in so far. Unbelievably, the dark cargo pants and polo shirt merely enhanced his attractiveness.

Thinking he was leaving, she caught her breath when he approached the bed. He stopped by the bedside table, snatched up the phone and calmly issued instructions before replacing the handset.

'A meal is being brought up to you,' he stated.

'Are you leaving?' she asked, and immediately wished back the needy words.

His gaze met hers for a moment before he turned away. 'It's better if I remove myself from here for now,' he rasped.

'Because you can't stand to be around me?'

He froze, then whirled towards her. 'Because our history of clashing tells me that we won't make it through a meal together without you voicing what's on your mind. Am I wrong?'

He wasn't. She wanted to discuss this *now*, get it out of the way, while he was intent on staging a diplomatic retreat. 'Even if you're not, I can't exactly stop you, can I?'

His nostrils flared. 'No, you can't. Rest, Maddie. I'll see you in a few hours.'

It's our wedding night, she wanted to scream. She swallowed the words. He didn't need to be reminded. That bleak look on his face told her he hadn't forgotten.

She watched him stride purposefully for the door, watched it shut with a decisive click behind him. Immediately Maddie felt as if a light switch had been thrown, plunging her world into darkness.

She'd made love to her husband on her wedding night without protection. And the first thing he had thought to mention was his dead fiancée. How clearer could it be that this marriage was doomed?

With shaking limbs, she sank back against the pillows, fighting for the breath that she couldn't catch properly in her lungs. She should never have agreed to marry him. She should never have agreed to this devil's bargain.

But then where would her father be?

Tears rose in her eyes as anvil weights of impossible choices pressed down on her.

She was still mired in despair when a soft knock sounded fifteen minutes later. The middle-aged woman who'd introduced herself as head housekeeper, when the staff had met them earlier, directed a younger maid, who pushed a silver trolley towards the bed.

Together they prepared a tray of food and a glass

of pure Montegovan spring water and set it in Maddie's lap. Belatedly, she wished she'd thrown on the robe when she caught their subtle stares. She mentally shrugged. At least the palace gossip wouldn't include speculation on whether her marriage had been consummated or not. She even managed a blush when the housekeeper picked up her discarded gown and carefully laid it on the sofa.

She picked at the fruit, flat bread and cold meats, drank the juice and sipped at the water. She suspected Remi had instructed the housekeeper to ensure she ate, because the older woman found an excuse to linger until Maddie had finished most of her plate before, smiling and curtsying, she departed.

Left alone with her thoughts, she was aware that a single one had emerged from the churning quagmire. The consequences of their actions went beyond Celeste and a marriage that seemed doomed even before it had begun.

If fate chose a different path for her, she would emerge from her wedding night carrying the future heir to the Montegovan throne. And one thing was very clear. Her new husband couldn't have been less thrilled about that prospect if he'd tried.

Remi paced his study, a single lit lamp the only illumination in the darkness. He embraced the gloom, let it amplify the sheer magnitude of what he'd let happen. He deserved this.

His carelessness was breathtaking. How could he have let himself be so blinded by lust that he'd forgotten himself at the very first opportunity?

Sure, he hadn't planned on making love to her again

that second time, but how was that an excuse when it had never happened before?

The truth was that he had lost himself.

Her beauty, her responsiveness, that tentative but determined exploration of her newly found sexuality... they'd all been a potent combination that had turned him on more than he would've believed possible before tonight.

He'd indulged himself, and in so doing had lost his mind. Spectacularly. And now he was faced with the possible consequences.

Maddie wasn't on birth control.

He'd read her medical report—knew a discussion had taken place with her new doctor for her to start after the wedding, in case she developed side effects.

The responsibility had therefore fallen squarely on him. How could he have failed so spectacularly?

There may be no consequences...

He wasn't reassured. He'd fallen at the first hurdle, just as he'd failed to come clean and admit that Celeste hadn't crossed his mind more than a handful of times since he'd returned to Montegova. That he'd been consumed with thinking about Maddie and finding ways to keep her to their agreement.

Because admitting it would have been too revealing? *Yes.*

Was tonight's slip a subconscious effort on his part to ensure she remained at his side? Even after vowing never to be careless with another's health again?

That unnerving thought froze him in place until the next one arrived hard on its heels.

Fatherhood. His new wife might well be carrying the next king or queen of Montegova. *His child.*

The reality shook through him, and then confounded him further by staggering him with need and...*hope*.

No. He couldn't possibly *want* this. Not when it could come at such a cost.

The hands he dragged through his hair shook. The notion unsettled him deeply. He stared into the middle distance, attempting to recall Celeste's face, remind himself of why he'd chosen this path. But he saw only Maddie, her anguish as she'd hurled accusations at him.

He swallowed, then gritted his teeth.

This couldn't happen again. If any consequences came of this night he would do everything in his power to ensure Maddie's safety. If nothing came of it—if fate saw fit to give him a second chance—he would do the right thing going forward. The *only* thing.

She'd slipped beneath his guard and under his skin. If he couldn't think clearly around her then his options were severely limited.

Skirting his desk, he sank heavily into the chair behind it, not sure which scenario he preferred. Both settled iron vices around his chest, strangling him. But he had no choice. It was the safest option.

He dragged his hands down his face, prolonging the moment for as long as possible.

Then he picked up the phone.

CHAPTER TEN

THE SUN WAS creeping beneath heavy silk curtains when Maddie opened her eyes. Anxiety and despair, coupled with the long, emotional wedding day, had finally taken their toll and she'd tumbled into a dreamless sleep just after midnight.

Heart hammering, she jerked upright, a fist-sized stone settling in her chest when her fears were confirmed. Remi hadn't returned to the suite. Or if he had, he'd chosen not to wake her.

Deep down, she knew she'd slept alone. Her senses were too attuned to him not to have noticed his presence.

Willing calmness to her thudding heart, she dragged herself out of bed. A quick inspection after using the bathroom showed only Remi's clothes in the dressing room. The thought of wearing the evening gown Remi had peeled off her body last night made the knots inside her tighten harder, so she retrieved the robe she'd never got round to wearing last night and shrugged it on.

With a deep breath she left the suite—to find a young maidservant hovering in the stunning hallway that looked even more spectacular in daylight than it had last night.

The girl, a few years younger than Maddie, gave a deep curtsy. 'Your Highness, I'm to escort you to your suite and ready you for breakfast with His Highness.'

Relief fizzed deep inside Maddie. A part of her had been afraid Remi had left the palace altogether.

Murmuring her thanks, she followed the girl to the only other door in the vast hallway. It turned out to be the suite adjoining Remi's. And inside the decidedly more feminine suite, set out in similar but more delicate amber tones, she found a whole new wardrobe ready for her.

After a quick shower, she selected a pale lemon sundress, slipped her feet into stylish mules and brushed her hair out. Light blusher to disguise her pale cheeks and a quick dab of lip-gloss and she was ready.

Remi sat at the head of a banquet-like dining table made of polished cherry wood, his fresh clothes and neatly combed hair evidence that he'd slept and dressed somewhere else.

The rigid expression that greeted her further evidenced the unsurpassable chasm between them.

'Good morning, Maddie. Did you sleep well?' he enquired tonelessly.

She forced a shrug. 'I slept. Let's leave it at that.'

His gaze flickered, but he remained silent as a fully uniformed butler approached. She knew she'd meet the same resistance if she attempted a discussion on an empty stomach, so she forced herself to eat a slice of toast and scrambled eggs, washed down with a cup of tea.

The moment she set her cutlery down Remi rose. 'We'll talk in my study,' he stated.

Her heart hollowed as she followed him down several magnificently decorated hallways and into a room decked out on three sides with floor-to-ceiling bookshelves, some holding first edition books.

But she wasn't there to gawp at the contents of Remi's ancestral library. She was there to discuss—perhaps even battle for—her marriage.

She hid her flinch when he shut the door and paced steadily to the window, looking out for a moment before facing her.

'What happened last night can never happen again.'

The heart dropped to her stomach and she sank into the nearest seat. 'It's too late to seek an annulment, Remi,' she replied, striving for a jovial tone that fell far short.

His lips firmed. 'That isn't quite the course of action I intend to take.'

'Then by all means enlighten me.'

'I'm aware that you were thrown into the deep end with the expediency of our wedding preparations. Now that it's over we can throttle things down a notch.'

'Isn't that what a honeymoon is for?'

He gave a half-nod. 'I'm proposing you extend that for longer, if you wish, by remaining here at the Amber Palace. It's not exactly a new concept. My mother stayed here when she was pregnant with me.'

'You mean stay here on my own…when you return to the Grand Palace?' she asked, sick premonition crawling over her skin.

There was a tight clench of his jaw. 'Yes,' he replied.

'We haven't been married for even twenty-four hours and already you want a separation? Because, let's face it, that's what you're proposing, isn't it?'

'Madeleine—'

She held up a staying hand. 'Don't try and couch it in diplomatic terms. We made love without protection and now you're freaking out.'

He drew in a long, harsh breath, his chest expanding along with his aura until she could see nothing, feel nothing but his overwhelming presence.

'I'm putting safeguards in place.'

'By banishing me?' she asked shakily.

A shadow passed over his face but his iron will held. 'We will continue to see each other. We just won't live under the same roof.'

She jumped up, unable to sit still any longer. 'What the hell are you so afraid of, Remi?' she demanded through a throat dry with panic.

For the longest time he remained silent. Then he exhaled. 'What happened to Celeste was my fault,' he confessed, in a voice devoid of any emotion.

'How?'

'She'd been suffering from migraines in the months before our wedding. Doctors had recommended tests but she'd pleaded with me to take her on a business trip. I was reluctant, but she talked me into it and I went against her doctors' advice. The headaches got worse when we were away. She suffered an aneurysm mid-flight on her way back home. If she'd stayed at home, or even returned a day earlier, the doctors might've saved her.'

'How can you blame yourself for that? You couldn't have known what would happen. And would she really want you to live in never-ending hell because she died?'

'What's the point of going through hell if you don't learn from it?' he bit out tersely.

'Learning from it is one thing. Shutting yourself off from experiencing anything else is another.'

'*Dio mio*. I'm trying to protect you, Maddie.' His voice was harsh. Ragged.

Her heart wanted to soften, to give in, but what would she be giving in to? A half-dead platonic marriage when she'd had a taste of how things could be if only he opened his heart?

'You can't control the future, Remi. No one can. You think you're protecting me, but what you're doing is insulating yourself from living a full life. I... I don't want that.'

His eyes narrowed. 'What does that mean?'

'It means you can't keep me in a cage, no matter how much you think you're justified in doing so.'

'You are a princess now. In a matter of weeks you'll be my queen. Like it or not, your new position means that in some ways you're constrained by your station. You can't do whatever you want, give in to frivolous dreams.'

'But I don't have to live in misery either, locked away in your Amber Palace. I won't play the out-of-sight-out-of-mind game with you.'

He dragged a hand through his hair, upsetting the neat strands. '*Dio*, none of this is a game. You could be pregnant.'

Her insides shook at the words, at the soul-shaking possibility, but she stood her ground. 'Even if I am, the last I heard pregnancy wasn't a prison sentence.'

'But it carries risks.'

'Walking down the street carries risks. I have first-hand knowledge of that, but I'm still here. Still alive. What if I'm *not* pregnant?'

His lips compressed. 'No protection is risk-free. And

since I've proved conclusively that my control is…lacking where you're concerned, it's best if we—'

'Don't you dare say it!' she blurted, distress shaking her voice.

His face closed completely. 'You will remember who you're addressing, Maddie. It's pointless to argue. My mind is made up. This is still only a marriage of convenience, which required consummation to make it lawful. Now we've done our duty there'll be no further intimacy between us.'

And just like that the loud clang of dungeon gates echoed, consigning the marriage she'd dared to hope she could have to a dark and lonely death.

She lifted her chin and looked him in the eyes. 'Very well, *Your Highness*. Since you don't need my permission to leave, I guess if I don't see you around I can assume you're gone.'

'Maddie—'

'If there's nothing else, I think I'll go and get acquainted with my new residence. I'm assuming, again, that your offer of a tour now falls to someone else?'

He gave a brisk nod. 'I have work to do.'

'Then don't let me keep you,' she replied stiffly.

He stayed exactly where he was, staring at her for a full minute before delivering one of his imperious nods. 'Your doctor will be in touch soon. We need to know one way or the other.'

With that, he turned on his heel and left the library.

Maddie sank onto the sofa, the breath knocked out of her lungs. And when she heard a helicopter land and then take off again half an hour later, she couldn't stop the sob that ripped from her throat or the torrent of tears that followed.

* * *

She didn't see Remi again for three long weeks, and although every other night she would hear him arrive in his helicopter, he would be gone by morning.

Of course, she mused bitterly. In all things he had to keep up appearances.

Maddie attempted to shrug off insidious despair in favour of getting to know her new home. After exploring every inch of the Amber Palace she spent hours in the elaborate maze, then discovered stables filled with thoroughbreds, stallions and two mares. With her pregnancy unconfirmed, Maddie could only admire them from afar as stable hands tended them.

Keeping herself busy prevented her from doing too much of the one thing that fed her despair—scouring social media for glimpses of Remi. With wedding fever abating, people were now turning their attention to the coronation. And from the looks of it, Remi was fully immersed in preparations—including touring the major cities of his kingdom.

His enigmatic responses when asked about the whereabouts of his wife had begun to fuel speculation of a possible royal baby on the way. She was therefore not surprised when he arrived with her doctor in tow on the twenty-second day.

Maddie was on the back terrace, overlooking the first of several tiered lawns as his helicopter settled on the helipad. Unable to help herself, she searched his face for signs that he'd missed her as much as she'd yearned for him, and deluded herself into thinking that she'd caught a single sizzling, ravenous look in his eyes before his expression gelled into regal neutrality.

'Madeleine,' he murmured stiffly as he brushed a kiss on her cheek.

Her heart quaked at that small contact, but she hardened her resolve. 'Your Highness,' she muttered back, and felt him stiffen. 'You should've called to tell me you were bringing the doctor. I would've told you not to bother.'

He tensed. 'Excuse me?'

She looked past him to the physician hovering at a respectful distance and pinned her smile in place. 'I'm not taking the test. We'll know one way or the other in a week or two anyway.'

'Madeleine—'

'I'm already being treated like fragile glass by the staff. I'd quite like to live in blissful ignorance for a little longer before I'm wrapped in cotton wool by the whole kingdom. So send the doctor away, Remi. Or I will. And while we're at it you should know my bags are packed. I'm returning to Playagova with or without your approval. I'm sure everyone's worked out that this honeymoon is over.'

He stared at her as if she'd grown two heads but she stood her ground.

'If that's what you wish—'

'It is. Thank you.'

The doctor was dispatched in a SUV and Maddie and Remi returned to the helicopter. During the thirty-five-minute flight Remi conducted phone call after phone call, including a particularly terse one.

'Whatever this is, you need to sort it out, Zak,' he said in English, before sliding back into Montegovan.

When he hung up his jaw was tense.

'Is everything all right with Zak?' she asked before she could stop herself.

'It'd better be. I have too much on my plate to deal with his issues.'

She shrugged. 'I only met him for a short time, but he seems capable of handling himself more than adequately.'

For the first time since boarding the helicopter, Remi flicked his gaze to her. It stayed and blazed. Her heart flipped over and her throat clogged with harrowing yearning, only for her to see the blaze cool seconds later.

'Since you seem to think you're up to handling your new role, we've been invited to my godmother's residence tomorrow evening. She's throwing a pre-coronation dinner in my honour.'

Nerves made her breath catch, but she swallowed them down. 'I… Of course.'

He nodded briskly as the helicopter landed. He alighted first, then turned to help her down the shallow steps. Again her breath caught, and this time when his gaze locked on hers she witnessed a reel of emotion in his eyes. Savage lust. Bleakness. Censure. Regret. All before the brick wall slammed down, shutting her out.

Numbness descended on Maddie, keeping her mercifully insulated as they entered the palace and were greeted by the exuberant staff. She forced herself to smile her way through accepting several bouquets of flowers from their children.

Even Queen Isadora approached as Maddie turned to head to her suite. 'Welcome home, *ma petite*. You're just in time to wish me well on my travels.'

Maddie's eyes widened. 'You're leaving?'

Queen Isadora nodded enthusiastically, her eyes shining with almost child-like glee. 'First stop New Zealand. I've always wanted to visit Hobbiton.'

Maddie smiled. 'I wish you very safe travels.'

'Thank you,' Queen Isadora replied. Her gaze flicked to where Remi stood, talking to his aide, and her face grew serious. 'Things may look bleak and daunting at present, but I've discovered that dogged perseverance reaps rich rewards.'

'I… I'll bear that in mind.'

The queen nodded, then briskly walked away.

Maddie dropped her head and buried her nose in a bouquet of chrysanthemums and peonies as she mulled over Queen Isadora's words.

She was startled out of her thoughts by the click of a camera. Although she knew she'd been caught unawares by the palace photographer, she dredged up a smile—which froze on her face when her eyes clashed with Remi's.

His gaze captured hers before dropping to her flat belly. For a tense moment he remained immobile, with a fierce look in his eyes that locked the air in her lungs. A second later he turned his back on her.

That numbing sensation still shrouded her when they drove through a set of iron gates manned by security guards the next evening.

They were barely out of the car when a thin, elegantly dressed woman Maddie had seen only in glossy magazines hurried towards them. She inhaled sharply.

'Your godmother is Margot Barringhall, the English Countess?'

'She's half-Montegovan. She's also my mother's best friend.' His tone was clipped. Resigned.

'You don't sound very happy about being here.'

'I'm fond of her, but Margot likes to play games.'

'What type of games?' she asked.

'You'll see,' he said cryptically.

'Remi, my dear, it's simply wonderful to see you.'

Arms outstretched, Margot hugged him, her smile widening as Remi kissed her on both cheeks.

'Maman wouldn't have forgiven me if I hadn't made time to see you before the coronation,' he drawled.

Margot laughed, but when her gaze swung to Maddie a second later her expression cooled. 'Ah, here's the blushing bride. Forgive me for leaving straight after your wedding ceremony. I had a prior engagement I simply couldn't break.' Her gaze dropped to Maddie's flat stomach. 'Even though it was all so…rushed I wish I'd been able to enjoy all of it. Anyway, welcome to the family. May I call you Madeleine?'

Remi was the only one who used her full name, and she was suddenly loath to grant that privilege to anyone else. She smiled stiffly. 'Maddie is fine.'

'I hope you're adjusting to your new role? It must be daunting.'

'I'm doing fine, but thank you for your concern,' Maddie replied, her insides tightening at the underlying dig. Margot wasn't talking about being a member of royalty. She meant Maddie's place in Remi's life.

Satisfied that her gibe had been delivered, Margot turned back to Remi. 'Come through—everyone's having drinks in the Blue Room.'

She claimed her godson's arm, and for a moment Maddie thought Remi would leave her behind. But his hand gripped hers, sending a bolt of electricity up her arm when their palms slid together.

She was so caught up in not reacting outwardly to that sizzling touch she barely had the wherewithal to gape at the roll call of celebrities and royals gracing Margot's stately home. But when Margot led them purposefully towards a trio of women who bore a striking resemblance to the beautiful Countess, Maddie felt her skin tighten.

'Remi, you remember Charlotte? She's returned from Sydney to accept a position with the UN. I managed to convince her that two years was long enough for her to be away. Who knows? She might take up a post here in Montegova.'

A telling look passed between mother and daughter.

'Welcome home,' Remi responded easily, but his smile held a cool edge. 'I'm sure my ministers can facilitate the appropriate meetings if required.'

Charlotte's face fell a fraction, but she hid it behind her glass of champagne as Remi turned his attention to the other two women, who were introduced as Sage and Violet, identical twins.

'Violet recently returned from New York too. She finished her internship with your brother. I've been trying to reach Zak for the letter of recommendation he promised, but he's been unavailable,' Margot complained.

Remi tensed, but before he could reply Violet inhaled sharply.

'*You've* been trying to reach Zak? I told you not to. I said I'd take care of it, Mother,' she admonished, her voice thin and shaky as her already pale cheeks blanched further.

A memory teased through Maddie's thoughts, reminding her that Violet was the woman she'd spotted on her way up the aisle. The woman Zak had tensed upon seeing.

Margot brushed her daughter away. 'His letter is important. You were under his guidance for six months and you've been home for two. It's time you took the next step in your career.'

Violet went paler. With an abruptly murmured excuse she rushed away.

Margot turned her blinding smile on Remi. 'Ah, here's the butler, come to announce dinner. Shall we go through?'

She looped both arms around Remi's elbow and pointedly led him away, leaving Maddie to follow. Margot Barringhall couldn't have made it clearer that she considered Maddie an outsider if she'd tried. Or the fact that she believed one of her daughters should have become the next Princess of Montegova.

Watching Charlotte Barringhall smile up at Remi as he pulled out her chair, Maddie felt the numbness surrounding her crack, to let in a sharp arrow that left her breathless with pain.

Her composure wasn't helped when over the next three hours nausea began to roll through her belly as rich course after decadent, rich course was ushered to the table. Suffering at the sight of the rich food, alongside Margot's less than subtle attempts to ostracise her, while indulgently nudging Charlotte and Remi into conversation, drained every last ounce of Maddie's poise.

For his part, Remi was the epitome of diplomacy, seemingly content to let his godmother have her way. But every now and then a jagged expression flitted across his face, driving that arrow deeper into Maddie's heart.

Over and over, she swore she wouldn't glance his way but, like a glutton for punishment, she repeatedly flicked her gaze to where he sat with Charlotte, their heads together, talking in low tones.

She couldn't deny they made a striking couple. Nor could she deny the acidic jealousy and wrenching anguish flaying her. Her gaze shifted, and she caught Sage staring at her. At the thinly veiled pity in the other woman's eyes Maddie tightened her fingers around her water glass.

Mercifully, dinner ended shortly after that. Sensing Remi coming her way, she sucked in a fortifying breath—only for her stomach to deliver an almighty heave.

'I need the ladies' room. Excuse me.' She hurried away, aware that his assessing gaze was firmly latched onto her.

Hunched over the water closet, Maddie knew it wasn't just the state of her marriage that was disturbing her stomach. Willing her body and soul to stop shaking, she staggered to the sink, rinsed her mouth and attempted to breathe around the anguish in her heart.

When the agony failed to ease, she turned on the tap and splashed water over her hands.

If she was pregnant—and a fierce instinct she couldn't suppress insisted she was—then this level of distress wasn't good for her unborn child.

She'd thought she knew what she'd let herself in for with this bargain, but Remi's coldness, Margot's callous dismissal, and the topsy-turvy awe and panic at the thought that she might be carrying the next Montegovan heir…

This was a whole new realm of agony.

Maddie was struggling for composure when the door opened and Violet rushed in. She froze at the sight of Maddie, dropping suspiciously teary eyes.

Maddie frowned in concern. 'Are you okay?'

Violet made a flouncy gesture eerily reminiscent of her mother, then paused, her gaze reconnecting with Maddie's.

'I know this is…' She stopped, cleared her throat. 'Has Remi said anything about Zak's whereabouts?' she blurted.

Maddie stopped herself from saying that she and Remi weren't on extended speaking terms. 'No. I'm sorry.'

'Oh, it's fine. Thanks.' Violet flashed a fake smile and left the bathroom.

About to follow her, Maddie reversed her direction abruptly as her belly dipped alarmingly. With a wretched sob she emptied the remaining contents of her stomach and was about to leave the stall when a pair of voices froze her exit.

'I don't know exactly where he dug her up, but perhaps you should warn him, Margot, before he brings the throne into disgrace. The story of her father is most unseemly. Who knows what he's passed down to her?'

Margot laughed. 'Remi doesn't need any warning. My godson's always been wise beyond his years. He'll wake up to his unfortunate error soon enough. Luckily divorce, even amongst royals, is commonplace these days.'

Maddie bit her fist to suppress her painful gasp.

'Are you sure?'

'Absolutely positive. He's doing this to secure his throne. If he's not single again by this time next year I'll buy you lunch at Claridge's. If he is, you can buy me dinner to celebrate my Charlotte's rightful place as the next queen.'

Both women laughed, and then just like that they went on to talk about something else, their decimation of Maddie's soul already a thing of the past.

Five excruciating minutes passed before she was once again alone, her heart in tatters.

She staggered out of the bathroom, her every sense screaming at the thought of returning to the dinner party. She wasn't ready for another episode of the Charlotte and Remi show. Wasn't ready to look into Remi's eyes and wonder if Margot was right. And, worse, wonder if he'd hate her even more for the secret growing into steady reality in her heart.

Spotting a large archway, she headed towards it. It opened up onto a terrace edged with a thick stone balustrade, beyond which lay an endless sweep of immaculate lawn.

Resting her elbows on the stone, Maddie took a deep breath—which immediately evaporated when the space between her shoulders began to tingle.

Awareness raced down her spine, relentlessly engulfing her whole body. The intensity of it shocked her into immobility, which was perhaps a blessing—because she didn't want to face her husband. The man who would soon gain another label—*the father of her child*.

Nor did she wish to face the undeniable fact that, despite the turbulence of their coming together, her feelings had only deepened unrelentingly, without regard to her anguish. Even more desperately, she didn't want him to take one look at her and *know everything*.

'Are you avoiding me, Maddie, or did you simply take a wrong turn when returning to me?' he rasped tautly.

She stayed facing forward, her frantic gaze fixed on the horizon as he prowled closer.

'I needed a breather from all that cloying fawning and shameless matchmaking. You should've warned me properly that I was going to spend the evening being insulted,' she said, her hands tightening around her clutch bag.

'You insisted you were ready to play at the deep end. I simply gave you the chance.'

His voice was close enough for her to feel his breath on her nape. To draw that fleeting contact into her being.

'Well, thanks for the lesson. I'll be suitably armed next time.'

'Turn around, Maddie. Have the courtesy to look at me when you address me,' he commanded tersely.

Praying that her last ounce of composure held, she swung around, felt a strand of hair escape its knot and slide against her cheek as she forced herself to meet his incisive gaze.

'Where exactly is Charlotte on your list? She *is* on the list, isn't she? She must be near the top if Margot refuses to acknowledge the wedding ring on my finger. Or do they all know this marriage is a sham?'

His face hardened. 'Keep your voice down.'

Her heart twisted. 'That's all you have to say?'

'No. I have a lot more to say. But this isn't the time or place.'

He closed the gap between them and lifted his hand

as if to touch the lock of escaped hair. But at the last moment his fist tightened and dropped.

Gut-wrenching anguish gripped her. 'Will it ever be?' she asked tremulously.

He took another step closer. Her breath strangled in her throat as his hands caged her against the balustrade.

His chest brushed hers. Maddie's nipples tightened. For an unshakeable moment they simply stared at each other, wrapped in a fraught little cocoon.

The tinkle of laughter and conversation from the party faded away. Her vision was filled with only Remi. When his head started to descend she stopped breathing, shameless anticipation holding her in place.

For the briefest moment another emotion shifted the savage hunger on his face. Powerful and visceral enough to make her flinch.

It was the same expression she'd witnessed yesterday, when he'd helped her from the helicopter, and again after her exchange with the Queen. It continued to blaze down at her as he slid one hand around her waist, tugged her into the hard column of his body.

With a will of their own her hands rose to his chest, splayed over hard muscle. Untamed hunger charged through his eyes, and with a groan he swooped and captured her mouth with his.

Deep, thorough and devastating, he explored her mouth with suppressed ferocity. In a rush of surrender she shamelessly parted her lips beneath his, let his tongue sweep over her lower lip in a blatant tasting that drew a moan from deep inside her.

Her belly grew hot and heavy with desire, and she gripped his nape and held on tight.

With a rough sound he slid his tongue into her mouth,

his breathing harsh as he adjusted his stance until there was no mistaking his level of arousal.

Maddie's whole body rippled with desire-soaked tremors. As if her reaction triggered his, his kiss deepened, his hand trailing up to boldly cup her heavy breast. With a helpless moan she pushed against him, nipped his bottom lip with her teeth. He exhaled harshly, muttering a charged curse against her lips.

She was so caught up in the kiss, in *him*, that it took a moment to notice that he'd stiffened.

He jerked away from her. *'Dio mio!'* he bit out, his hands falling from her waist.

She dropped her hands, shifted sideways away from him as she gulped in several breaths. The sound of the guests' laughter reminded her where she was.

Remi took another step back, the cloak of diplomacy settling on his face once more. But beneath that look she saw lingering anguished regret. As if he was berating himself for the very thing he'd instigated.

A breeze swept up from the garden, chilling her body. She rubbed at her arms but the cold just intensified.

'If we're done with the lesson, can we leave now?' she asked through stiff lips.

'Of course.' His tone was devoid of inflexion, his demeanour staid as he led her back inside.

Neither of them spoke for the duration of the journey back to the palace and the long minutes it took them to walk back to their adjoining suites. Expecting him to escort her to her bedroom door, Maddie felt her skin grow tight with apprehension when he veered into his living room and strode to the arched windows over-looking the landscaped gardens.

A stone jumped into her throat at the flash of bleak-ness on his face. His gaze stayed in the middle distance for the longest time before a hard edge replaced the bleakness. When he turned to her, she held her breath, a part of her almost afraid of what he would say.

'What happened on the balcony shouldn't have hap-pened.'

Despite the staccato precision of his revelation his anguish was unmistakable. Her insides shrivelled as she watched him wrestle that telling emotion.

There was only one reason behind this disclosure. *Guilt*.

The sharpest knife pierced her at the thought that he would never stop loving his dead fiancée. Hard on its heels, though, came anger.

'It was just a kiss, Remi. You won't burn in hell for it.'

His jaw clenched. 'Nevertheless, I gave you my word—'

'I didn't ask for your word, so don't you dare beg my forgiveness because you think you're dishonour-ing your fiancée's memory. Or is it something else? Do you hate the fact that you liked it? That your own wife turns you on?'

Icy fury blasted through his eyes. 'Madeleine—'

She affected a shaky shrug, despite the deep tremors coursing through her body. 'You're an intelligent man, Remi. If this meant nothing to you, you wouldn't be so affected by it. And you wouldn't deign to speak to me, never mind attempt to dissect it.'

Grey eyes pinned her as he exhaled harshly. 'You think you have a handle on what makes me tick?'

She laughed. 'No, I don't. I'm just going on the evidence before me. We made love. You *loved* it. Then immediately retreated. Tonight we kissed. You were *transported*. Now you hate me—and hate yourself for responding to a commoner like me.'

He didn't move a muscle but he seemed to grow before her, every inch of his majestic being bristling with affront. 'To hate you I would have to be invested in you, even a small fraction. I'm not. And in future I'll thank you not to attempt to psychoanalyse me.'

The tears she'd striven to hold back all night threatened to break through as the gnawing, traumatising truth took root inside her.

She couldn't save a marriage that had been doomed from inception. She was better off cutting her losses.

'You won't need to worry about that. Not any more,' she said, a heavy wave of desolation sweeping over her.

She wanted to succumb, wanted to surrender to its oblivion. But she forced herself to stay on her feet as he pinned her with his gaze.

'What's that supposed to mean?'

'It means I won't be attending the charity polo match tomorrow. In fact you won't have to suffer my presence for much longer.'

He stiffened, but she caught the tremor that shook through his body. 'What exactly are you trying to tell me, Madeleine?'

She swallowed, knowing she couldn't bury her head in the sand any longer. She was pregnant with Remi's baby. The heir to the Montegovan throne. Finally accepting it filled her with both trepidation and acute joy. She needed time alone to process the news.

'I'm trying to tell you that I think your worst fears have come true,' she announced.

Remi froze, a wave of colour leaving his face as his eyes grew a turbulent black. His fists tightened at his sides and a harsh breath was ripped from his throat before his gaze lanced over her, pausing for one ragged second on her belly before lifting to clash with hers.

'Yes,' she confirmed the question in his eyes. 'I haven't taken the test yet, but...well, call it female intuition. I'm carrying your child, Remi. Tomorrow we'll know for certain, but at least you'll have tonight to start planning how you can truly separate me from your life.'

Her voice broke shamefully, raggedly, on the last words. Unable to withstand the agony any longer, she hurried into her own suite.

She heard him follow, heard him pause on the threshold of their adjoining rooms. He'd never crossed it—not once since they'd said their vows. She whirled to face him as he stepped through and stopped in front of her.

His hands rose as if to touch her. She jerked away. 'What are you doing?'

His face closed but determination blazed from his eyes. 'We need to talk, discuss—'

'Nothing that can't wait till morning,' she interjected bleakly, shifting her gaze away from the vibrant skin beneath his collarbone, from the towering vitality of this man who would never be hers.

She turned away. The result of fake smiling all evening while dealing with Margot and his coolly detached attitude had triggered a dull headache. She tossed her wrap and clutch on the sofa and massaged her temples with tired fingers.

'What's wrong?' he demanded sharply.

Maddie started, unaware he'd followed her. For a tense moment she stared at him, her brain frozen at his closeness.

'I have a headache. I also have to wake up early to talk to my father. I'd rather not do so with a headache…'

It was the first conversation she'd have with her father since she'd left England and he'd gone to Switzerland. She didn't want to miss it. Right now he felt like her only tether to the real world.

Her words trailed off as he strode past her and headed for her bathroom. Curious despite her breaking heart, she stayed put.

He returned with a pill bottle, shook out two tablets. 'Take these,' he instructed gruffly, handing her a glass of water.

'I'm fine—'

'Take them, Maddie. It's a low dose. It won't affect you or the—' He stopped, clenched his jaw.

Her heart lurched painfully. 'The *baby*, Remi. Not saying the word won't make it any less real.'

He inhaled sharply. 'You think I want to pretend it doesn't exist?'

The question was a stunned, ragged demand. One that drew a cloak of shame over her for even daring to voice the thought.

Unable to answer, or to stem the flare of hope inside her, she took the pills, her stomach pitching as her fingers brushed his warm palm.

He waited until she'd swallowed them before he returned to the living room. Then he turned on her. 'Why didn't you tell me you weren't feeling well?'

'It's just a headache, Remi.'

'Headaches can be an indicator of other things,' he

stressed, his tone deep and gravel-rough as his gaze dropped to her now healed arm.

She stared at him, her heart wrenching for him despite her own agony. 'I'm not being blithe or dismissive, Remi. It's just a tension headache. A good night's sleep will take care of it.'

He didn't reply, and the intense look in his eyes told her he wanted to argue. Eventually he gave a terse nod, then strode to her bed and pulled back the cover. For a long moment he stared at the sheets, seemingly lost in thought. Then he muttered a thick, 'Goodnight,' and walked into his own suite.

An hour later her headache was gone, but her desolation had grown exponentially when she started at the sound of their adjoining door opening.

Remi stood framed in the doorway, still dressed but minus his dinner jacket. His hair was in disarray, as if he'd spent the last hour running his fingers through it, and his eyes were dark pools of intensity.

Her heart leapt into her throat, as she blinked back the tears in her eyes. 'Remi—?'

'I won't leave this,' he said tersely. 'Not another night. Fate hasn't been good to me when I've let things be, Madeleine. You tell me I'm to be a father. Whatever that entails we tackle this. *Tonight.*'

CHAPTER ELEVEN

SHE REMAINED FROZEN, struck dumb, as he strode determinedly to her bedside. Fervently he searched her features. His fingers flexed at his sides but he didn't reach for her.

'How do you feel?'

Her fingers tightened on the luxurious bedspread as she fought to keep her crazy pulse from leaping out of control at his breath-stealing masculine beauty. He was barred to her, she reminded herself. Completely and conclusively. Somewhere in the last hour she'd accepted that her time with Remi was limited. This was her last chance to hoard memories of him.

She licked nervous lips and forced herself to meet his gaze. 'I'm fine. The headache is gone.'

Those all-seeing eyes lingered, dropped to her mouth, and just like that the atmosphere thickened. But this time it was overlaid with an intensity unlike anything she'd ever known.

'Fate hasn't been good to me...'

'Whatever that entails, we tackle this...'

'What...what exactly do you want to tackle?'

He didn't speak immediately, simply continued to watch her with a spine-jarring ferocity that stole her breath.

Time ticked by. The merest frown creased his eyebrow before his face slowly went slack. It was the kind of expression triggered by dawning realisation. Or emotionless calculation.

Self-preservation screamed at Maddie to turn away, to hide from that look in his eyes. But she couldn't move.

Whatever the future held, it was time for her to face it.

Remi stared down at his wife, the staggering realisation of the last hour slaying him anew.

The last three weeks without her had been hell, with each day worse than the last, because she was the missing part of him he'd never even known he'd lost. He'd planned to tell her that tomorrow. To lay it all on the line when things weren't so volatile between them. But he hadn't even been able to undress, never mind find any semblance of respite.

The staggering notion that time was slipping through his fingers had been overwhelming. And, really, hadn't he wasted enough time? Hadn't he known from that moment she got into his car that Madeleine Myers possessed the ability to shift his world off its axis in the most profound, life-changing way?

How could he have slept, knowing that tomorrow might be too late? That he might lose the woman who held his heart, held his child within her womb?

He shifted his gaze over her face again, fighting the trepidation in his chest, scrambling for words adequate enough to combat that look in her eyes he knew didn't bode well for him. For weeks he'd pushed her away. What if...?

'Madeleine...'

'What is it, Remi? What did you come to say to me?'

He took a long, ragged breath. 'That I'm a husband who has neglected his wife for far too long. I won't be making that mistake again.'

Her breath shook but she held his gaze. 'If this is about confirming my pregnancy, you can go ahead and call the doctor. Neither of us is going to get any sleep anyway. It's best we find out now. But you should know that after that things will change, Remi.'

His heart dropped into his stomach, ice and heat engulfing him simultaneously. He wanted to prolong the eventuality. Wanted to speak the words tripping on his tongue. But for the first time in his life the right words wouldn't form. So he picked up the phone and summoned his physician.

He arrived within half an hour. Endless minutes during which his words still remained locked in his throat, his fate hanging on a knife-edge.

'Royal protocol dictates that the test result be as accurate as possible. A blood test is the most definitive,' Remi heard the physician tell her.

'Right. Of course. And how long before…?'

Remi's vocal cords finally unfroze. 'A matter of hours, I believe?' he replied, his heart racing frantically.

Maddie's breath caught, her gaze finding his. 'Are you…are you going to stay?'

Remi nodded, walked to her side on legs that felt unsteady. 'If it pleases you, I'd very much like us to find out together.'

Maddie willed her heart to stop racing but that look she'd caught in his eyes a moment ago, that flash of deep yearning, continued to replay in her mind. Of course now he stood by her side the look was gone, his expression stoic as the doctor went to work.

The moment he was done Maddie rose from the bed. It was one thing to experience the distance between them from afar; it was another having him right next to her and still feeling as if nothing could breach the wasteland.

'Are you all right?' he asked.

She gave a bitter laugh. 'Do you care?'

'Of course I care.'

He was moving even closer. She knew it because his scent—the unique ice and earth scent she'd missed so much that it was a constant ache inside her—was wrapping itself around her, seeping into her ravenous senses.

Throat-grating laughter spilled again. 'You came to my room over an hour ago and you're yet to say what you came to say. I'm guessing that whatever it is isn't important to you any more.'

She felt him stop behind her. Beneath her night-slip and the dressing gown she'd thrown on her body strained for his with a shocking hunger.

'It's important, Maddie. Probably the most important thing I'll ever say.'

She whirled to face him, anger and despair and wild, unstoppable craving ripping her apart. 'Really? Then what's stopping you? Are you afraid you'll hurt me more than you already have? Whatever it is, say it and be done with it. Or would you prefer me to bow and scrape and pretend civility? Will that help you keep that control you so sorely lack around me? Or have you mastered that already in the weeks you've refused to touch me?'

His face started to tighten but he shook his head. 'I'm beginning to think that was a mistake.'

'Well, bully for you,' she lashed out.

'Maddie…'

His voice was as shaken as the gaze that dropped to her flat belly. His throat worked but he couldn't seem to form more words. He whirled away from her, then reversed direction. Shaky hands cupped her jaw.

Maddie's heart cracked open, but she swallowed the pain. She needed to do this, get through this. 'Something's going to change,' she said.

He tensed. 'What?'

'My father's out of isolation. After I talk to him in the morning I plan to go and see him as soon as I can. And…and then I'm going home—back to London.'

Anguish darkened his eyes and he grew another shade paler. 'No,' he rasped. 'You can't go. You can't leave me. I won't let you.'

The peculiar note in his voice snagged something hard in her chest. 'You can't keep me, Remi. Not like this. We won't survive as long as Celeste—'

'I haven't thought about Celeste since the first time I kissed you,' he interjected thickly.

She gasped. 'What?'

Firm hands grasped her shoulders as his eyes blazed with a new, terrifyingly intense light. 'You seem to think she dictates my every move. I accept that losing her the way I did affected me…badly…but from the moment you got into my car the only time I've thought about her is when I attempted to use her memory to stop myself from feeling what I feel for you.'

A deep tremble surged from the soles of her feet. 'And what *do* you feel for me?'

The hands that rose from her shoulders to cup her cheeks weren't quite steady. 'More than I wanted to at first. More than I could deal with. And I admit it terrified me how much I craved you,' he growled.

'You closed yourself off from me easily enough.'

His low laugh was gruff and self-deprecating. 'You think it was easy? Leaving you was the hardest thing I've ever done. Staying away was even harder. Why do you think I came back every other day?'

'Because you wanted to keep up appearances?'

He uttered a pithy curse under his breath. 'You should know by now that when it comes to you, appearances matter very little to me. No, I returned because even though I tried to stay away from you I yearned for you with every breath. I had to be near you even if I couldn't be with you. And I didn't walk away because of your strength. I walked away because of my weakness. I'm in love with you, Madeleine. But I put you in an impossible position and coerced you into this marriage… and I've spent every waking moment since then fighting my conscience against letting you go. Slipping up with protection seemed to be another sign that I wasn't doing right by you.'

'So…you intend to set me free?' she whispered raggedly.

'That was my intention the morning after our wedding night…for all of half a second. But to do that I'd have to rip my own heart out because you're so imbedded in it. I can't live without you, Maddie. I was relieved when you insisted on coming back to the palace. But having you close without having you is torture. So I'm here to plead for a fresh start. To see if there is a way we can start over regardless of what the test results show.'

His nostrils flared as he inhaled sharply. 'That means you're not allowed to leave me,' he stated.

A tremulous smile broke free. 'I'm not, am I?'

A mixture of pleading and determination stamped his face. 'I'll do whatever you want. We can return to the Amber Palace or we can live here. The staff tell me you've grown attached to the maze at the Amber Palace.'

'It was a place to lose myself for a few hours when I missed you so badly.'

Silver-grey eyes lit up with a churning of emotions so vivid her breath caught. 'I love you, Maddie. Give me another chance. I vow never to be separated from you again.'

'I'll have you on one condition, Remi.'

He inhaled sharply. 'Name it and it's yours.'

'Kiss me, Remi. Love me. Make me yours again. Please.'

He kissed her with a ferocious hunger that filled the ache in her heart. And when he caught her hand and led her through to his suite Maddie went willingly.

She let him take off her clothes and lay her on his bed. When he undressed and pulled her into his arms, she slid her hand over his jaw.

'Remi?'

'Si, amore dea?'

'I love you, too.'

His eyes blazed bright for endless moments before he blinked. 'Will you stay with me? Be my queen? Reign by my side?'

'On one condition…'

He caught and kissed the palm of her hand. 'Celeste's belongings were returned to her parents the morning after our wedding. There's no trace of her in our home and the staff are under strict instructions to speak as much or as little about her as you dictate. She was a part of me, but she's in my past now. Your strength, your devotion, your courageous challenges and the way you never back down are what I yearn for in my life. What I hope to be privileged enough to receive every day for as long as we live.'

Tears clogged her throat. 'Oh, Remi.'

'It's my turn to demand a kiss.'

She wrapped willing and loving arms around him and gave herself up to him. Then silence reigned as they gave in to bliss.

Two hours later, freshly showered, they descended the grand staircase hand in hand.

To the news from the doctor that she was indeed carrying the Montegovan heir.

Remi promptly swept her off her feet and carried her back upstairs.

After calling his mother to tell her the news, they called her father. Hearing him happy and healthy brought fresh tears to her eyes. She rang off with a promise to visit with Remi, after which she slid back into her husband's arms.

'Are you ready to be a father?'

Eyes feverish with love consumed her as his hand splayed over her belly. 'With you by my side, I can face anything.'

'God, how can love hurt and make me so happy at the same time?'

'Because it's the most powerful emotion of all. And I'm blessed to have yours.'

'I love you. For ever, Remi.'

'Siempre, mia regina.'

EPILOGUE

MADDIE WATCHED HER husband swim towards where she lay on a lounger next to the pool at the Amber Palace.

At five months pregnant, she knew her belly was rounded enough to make her state visible—a fact demonstrated by her husband when he launched himself out of the pool and immediately crossed to her side, his gaze lingering lovingly on her belly.

'Have I told you how breathtaking you look?'

'Not since this morning, no,' she said with a mock pout.

He dropped to his knees beside her, one hand gliding over her swollen stomach as he leaned down to kiss her. 'I can barely catch my breath from how beautiful you are, *dea mia*,' he said gruffly when he lifted his head after a thorough, soul-shaking kiss.

'You take my breath away too, my noble king.'

King Remirez of Montegova had taken to his new title and role with aplomb, and his people were showering even more adoration upon him now than they had at his coronation three months ago.

But it was when Maddie used his title like this in private moments that he loved it most.

His eyes darkened now, an arrogant smile curving

his mouth when a thorough scrutiny showed what his focused attention had done to her body. His gaze lingered on her peaked nipples and racing pulse before coming back to hers.

He started to reach for her again, then groaned when his phone rang.

He answered, his features growing irritated as the conversation continued. Then he hung up abruptly and tossed the phone aside.

She caught his hand, wove her fingers through his. 'Is everything okay?'

His lips compressed. 'It looks like Jules isn't the only brother causing waves. Zak isn't answering his phone…again…and Violet Barringhall seems to have disappeared.'

'What? Is she…? Do you need to inform the authorities?'

He shook his head. 'My security team informs me they're both unharmed, and curiously in the same Caribbean location.' His tone was more irritated than furious.

'You think they're together?'

'Most likely. I can only surmise that they wish to remain incommunicado. But, whatever they're up to, I'm not going to let them ruin this moment.'

'Oh? And what moment is that?'

'The most perfect of moments—which is every second I spend with you, my wife, my heart. And with our son. With this love that fills my heart each day.'

He kissed her again, his hand resting on her belly. And, as if fate itself had decreed it, their child gave his first ever kick.

Maddie gasped, tears of joy filling her eyes. 'Oh, my God—did you feel that?'

Remi's smile was shaky. '*Si*. That was our son, confirming what I already know. That we are blessed beyond words. That each day you hold my heart in your hands is a lifetime I would never wish to be without. I love you, Madeleine.'

'I love you, my king. Always.'

* * * * *

If you enjoyed
Crown Prince's Bought Bride
by Maya Blake,
you're sure to enjoy these other
Conveniently Wed! stories!

Sicilian's Bride for a Price
by Tara Pammi
Claiming His Christmas Wife
by Dani Collins
My Bought Virgin Wife
by Caitlin Crews
The Sicilian's Bought Cinderella
by Michelle Smart

Available now!

#3709 SPANIARD'S BABY OF REVENGE
by Clare Connelly

Antonio plans to persuade innocent Amelia to sell her shares in his rival's business. But he doesn't plan on their intense connection—and is stunned to discover their nine-month consequence. To secure his child, he'll make Amelia his wife!

#3710 CLAIMING MY UNTOUCHED MISTRESS
by Heidi Rice

Edie agreed to clear her family's debts by posing as my temporary mistress, helping expose my business rivals. Yet Edie's innocence is a temptation I couldn't have imagined. Our chemistry is spectacular—now I'll claim Edie for more than pleasure!

#3711 REUNITED BY A SHOCK PREGNANCY
by Chantelle Shaw

Sienna should not be secretly attending her ex-husband's wedding. Until she realizes Nico isn't the groom... But when he follows her, their burning fire reignites, leaving Sienna shockingly pregnant with the Italian's child!

#3712 THE BILLIONAIRE'S VIRGIN TEMPTATION
by Michelle Conder

Ruby is stunned when Sam sweeps her into an anonymous seduction! But when Ruby realizes Sam is her new boss, and they're left stranded together, his forbidden touch could be powerful enough to unravel Ruby forever...

YOU CAN FIND MORE INFORMATION ON UPCOMING HARLEQUIN® TITLES, FREE EXCERPTS AND MORE AT WWW.HARLEQUIN.COM.

HPCNM0319RB

*Walking into my casino, Edie Spencer seemed like a
spoiled heiress—until she agreed to clear her family's
debts by posing as my temporary mistress. My plan? To
use her to expose my business rivals. Yet discovering
Edie's innocence has led to greater temptation than I
could have imagined. Our chemistry is spectacular—
now I'll claim Edie for so much more than pleasure!*

*Read on for a sneak preview of
Heidi Rice's next story,*
Claiming My Untouched Mistress.

"Your sister told me exactly how deep your financial troubles go,"
I said. "I have a possible solution."

"What is it?" Edie said, desperation plain on her face.

"Would you consider working for me?" I asked.

"You're...you're offering me a job?"

She sounded so surprised, I found my lips curving in amusement
again.

"As it happens, I am hosting an event at my new estate near
Nice at the end of the month. I could use your skills as part of the
team I'm putting together."

"What exactly do you need me to do?" she said, her eagerness
a sop to my ego.

"The guests I am inviting are some of the world's most powerful
businessmen and women." I outlined the job. "They have all shown
an interest in investing in the expansion of the Allegri brand. The
event is a way of assessing their suitability as investors. As part of
the week, I will be offering some recreational poker events. These

people are highly competitive and they enjoy games of chance. What they don't know is that how they play poker tells me a great deal more about their personalities and their business acumen—and whether we will be compatible—than a simple profit-and-loss portfolio of their companies. But I find that successful people, no matter how competitive they are, are also smart enough to know that they cannot best me at a poker table. So I need someone who does not intimidate them, but who can observe how they play and make those assessments for me." I kept my eyes on her reaction, surprised myself by how much I wanted her to say yes.

My attraction to her might be unexpected, but I had spent a lifetime living by my wits and never doubting my instincts. When I had originally considered giving her a hosting position I'd been aware of the possible fringe benefits for both of us and I didn't see why that should change. She had made it very clear she was more than happy to blur the lines between employer and lover, and all her responses made it equally clear she desired me as much as I desired her.

"I'll pay you four thousand euros for the fortnight," I said, to make her position clear. This was a genuine job, and a job she would be very good at. "Joe can brief you on each of the participants—and what I need to know about them. If you do a good enough job, and your skills prove as useful as I'm expecting them to be, I would consider offering you a probationary position."

She blinked several times, her skin now flushed a dark pink, but didn't say anything.

"So do you want the job?" I asked, letting my impatience show, annoyed by the strange feeling of anticipation. Why should it matter to me if she declined my offer?

"Yes, yes," she said. "I'll take the job."